Shakespeare's Cats

The Complete Sonnets For The Literary Cat Lover

William Shakespeare
the Editors of Mango Media
and **Sir Falstaff**

GRANADILLA PRESS

Maria A. Llorens/Mango Media, Inc.
100 Miracle Mile, Suite 200
Miami, FL 33134
www.mangomedia.us

Publisher's Note: This is a work of nonfiction. Names, characters, places, and incidents are based on historical fact. Locales and public names are sometimes used for informative purposes. Any resemblance to actual people, living or dead, or to businesses, companies, events, institutions, or locales is completely coincidental.

Shakespeare's Cats: The Complete Sonnets for the Literary Cat Lover
Maria A. Llorens/Mango Media Inc. -- 1st ed.
ISBN 978-1-63353-027-0

I am as vigilant as a cat to steal cream.

~Sir Falstaff, *Henry IV*

TABLE OF CONTENTS

Friends and Family

" *Pity the world, or else this glutton be*
To eat the world's due, by the grave and thee "

Sonnet 1

From fairest creatures we desire increase,
That thereby beauty's rose might never die,
But as the riper should by time decease,
His tender heir might bear his memory:
But thou contracted to thine own bright eyes,
Feed'st thy light's flame with self-substantial fuel,
Making a famine where abundance lies,
Thy self thy foe, to thy sweet self too cruel:
Thou that art now the world's fresh ornament,
And only herald to the gaudy spring,
Within thine own bud buriest thy content,
And, tender churl, mak'st waste in niggarding:
   Pity the world, or else this glutton be,
   To eat the world's due, by the grave and thee.

what it means

This sonnet begins the "procreation" sonnets (numbers 1-17) and introduces the Fair Youth character, whose real-world identity has been widely debated. Here, Shakespeare encourages him to marry and bear children so that the world may share in his beauty after he is gone.

Sonnet 3

Look in thy glass and tell the face thou viewest
Now is the time that face should form another;
Whose fresh repair if now thou not renewest,
Thou dost beguile the world, unbless some mother.
For where is she so fair whose uneared womb
Disdains the tillage of thy husbandry?
Or who is he so fond will be the tomb
Of his self-love, to stop posterity?
Thou art thy mother's glass and she in thee
Calls back the lovely April of her prime;
So thou through windows of thine age shalt see,
Despite of wrinkles, this thy golden time.
But if thou live, remembered not to be,
Die single and thine image dies with thee.

what it means

The youth is told that he reflects his mother's
beauty, and that he should have children so
that they may remind him of his prime
once he is old.

fact

Shakespeare grew up in Stratford-
upon-Avon, a small town about 2
hours northwest of London.

Sonnet 4

Unthrifty loveliness, why dost thou spend
Upon thy self thy beauty's legacy?
Nature's bequest gives nothing, but doth lend,
And being frank she lends to those are free:
Then, beauteous niggard, why dost thou abuse
The bounteous largess given thee to give?
Profitless usurer, why dost thou use
So great a sum of sums, yet canst not live?
For having traffic with thy self alone,
Thou of thy self thy sweet self dost deceive:
Then how when nature calls thee to be gone,
What acceptable audit canst thou leave?
  Thy unused beauty must be tombed with thee,
  Which, used, lives th' executor to be.

what it means

Here Shakespeare tells the youth that Nature
only lends him his beauty, with the intended
purpose to profit the world with children.
He compares him to a moneylender
who, rather than share his money
and profit from moneylending,
keeps it for himself.

fact

Shakespeare was educated in
his youth, but probably not past
his early teens. Back then, grade-
schoolers were learning Latin and
classical literature.

Sonnet 6

Then let not winter's ragged hand deface,
In thee thy summer, ere thou be distilled:
Make sweet some vial; treasure thou some place
With beauty's treasure ere it be self-killed.
That use is not forbidden usury,
Which happies those that pay the willing loan;
That's for thy self to breed another thee,
Or ten times happier, be it ten for one;
Ten times thy self were happier than thou art,
If ten of thine ten times refigured thee:
Then what could death do if thou shouldst depart,
Leaving thee living in posterity?
Be not self-willed, for thou art much too fair
To be death's conquest and make worms thine heir.

what it means

Shakespeare asks the Fair Youth to not let winter
set upon the summer of his beauty. Death can
only be defeated through children, as they
will continue his legacy. If not, only the
worms in his grave will be his heir.

fact

Shakespeare inherited a coat of
arms when his father died in 1601,
a symbol separating him from
British commoners. The seal had
a spear and a falcon. So, when his
father died, he officially became a
gentleman.

Sonnet 8

Music to hear, why hear'st thou music sadly?
Sweets with sweets war not, joy delights in joy:
Why lov'st thou that which thou receiv'st not gladly,
Or else receiv'st with pleasure thine annoy?
If the true concord of well-tuned sounds,
By unions married, do offend thine ear,
They do but sweetly chide thee, who confounds
In singleness the parts that thou shouldst bear.
Mark how one string, sweet husband to another,
Strikes each in each by mutual ordering;
Resembling sire and child and happy mother,
Who, all in one, one pleasing note do sing:
   Whose speechless song being many, seeming one,
   Sings this to thee: 'Thou single wilt prove none.

what it means

The theme continues, and here Shakespeare uses
music as his argument. He comments that
music, like a family, is harmonious because
each string and tune works in tandem.
The youth, he says, is sad while
listening to music because he
does not want to submit to this
harmony. But, he must,
because he will die.

fact

Shakespeare had three
children—Susanna, Judith and
Hamnet. His son Hamnet died at
age 11, but it has been suggested
that **Hamlet** is named after him.
Not all scholars agree on this.

Sonnet 9

Is it for fear to wet a widow's eye,
That thou consum'st thy self in single life?
Ah! if thou issueless shalt hap to die,
The world will wail thee like a makeless wife;
The world will be thy widow and still weep
That thou no form of thee hast left behind,
When every private widow well may keep
By children's eyes, her husband's shape in mind:
Look what an unthrift in the world doth spend
Shifts but his place, for still the world enjoys it;
But beauty's waste hath in the world an end,
And kept unused the user so destroys it.
No love toward others in that bosom sits
That on himself such murd'rous shame commits.

what it means

The poet asks the youth if he's afraid of making his future wife a widow. If so, it is a silly belief, as the entire world will endure widowhood at his death. Children, at least, would serve as a comfort to the world.

fact

The Bard has no direct living descendants. His last descendant was a granddaughter named Elizabeth who did not have children. His sister, Joan Hart, had four children and still has living descendants today.

Sonnet 11

As fast as thou shalt wane, so fast thou grow'st
In one of thine, from that which thou departest;
And that fresh blood which youngly thou bestow'st,
Thou mayst call thine when thou from youth convertest.
Herein lives wisdom, beauty, and increase;
Without this folly, age, and cold decay:
If all were minded so, the times should cease
And threescore year would make the world away.
Let those whom nature hath not made for store,
Harsh, featureless, and rude, barrenly perish:
Look whom she best endowed, she gave the more;
Which bounteous gift thou shouldst in bounty cherish:
　　She carved thee for her seal, and meant thereby,
　　Thou shouldst print more, not let that copy die.

what it means

Similar to Sonnet 1, Sonnet 11 says the world desires more of what is good. Leave then, Shakespeare says, the fate of death to sullen, ugly souls. Your beauty should be copied many times and serve as a gift to the world.

fact

Shakespeare's works have been translated into more than 80 languages. As of September 2014, the United Kingdom Secretary of State for Culture, Media and Sport intends to donate 1.5 million pounds for the first translation of Shakespeare's complete works into Mandarin Chinese.

Sonnet 13

O! that you were your self; but, love, you are
No longer yours, than you your self here live:
Against this coming end you should prepare,
And your sweet semblance to some other give:
So should that beauty which you hold in lease
Find no determination; then you were
Yourself again, after yourself's decease,
When your sweet issue your sweet form should bear.
Who lets so fair a house fall to decay,
Which husbandry in honour might uphold,
Against the stormy gusts of winter's day
And barren rage of death's eternal cold?
O! none but unthrifts. Dear my love, you know,
You had a father: let your son say so.

what it means

This is the first sonnet that makes a direct
declaration of love, but it still continues the
theme that the youth's beauty should be
shared with future children. They will
serve as a barrier against "death's
eternal cold."

fact

Many of Shakespeare's works were
not printed in his lifetime, including
Macbeth and *Julius Caesar*.

Sonnet 14

Not from the stars do I my judgement pluck;
And yet methinks I have Astronomy,
But not to tell of good or evil luck,
Of plagues, of dearths, or seasons' quality;
Nor can I fortune to brief minutes tell,
Pointing to each his thunder, rain and wind,
Or say with princes if it shall go well
By oft predict that I in heaven find:
But from thine eyes my knowledge I derive,
And, constant stars, in them I read such art
As truth and beauty shall together thrive,
If from thyself, to store thou wouldst convert;
  Or else of thee this I prognosticate:
  Thy end is truth's and beauty's doom and date.

what it means

Shakespeare here states that the youth's eyes are
more beautiful and foretell more than the stars.
And while he cannot predict disease or bad
weather, he finds knowledge of beauty
and truth in them. So, of course, the
youth should make babies or
he'll die alone.

fact

A rare original print of Shakespeare's
plays, called a First Folio, was sold for
over $5 million in 2006.

Sonnet 15

When I consider every thing that grows
Holds in perfection but a little moment,
That this huge stage presenteth nought but shows
Whereon the stars in secret influence comment;
When I perceive that men as plants increase,
Cheered and checked even by the self-same sky,
Vaunt in their youthful sap, at height decrease,
And wear their brave state out of memory;
Then the conceit of this inconstant stay
Sets you most rich in youth before my sight,
Where wasteful Time debateth with decay
To change your day of youth to sullied night,
And all in war with Time for love of you,
As he takes from you, I engraft you new.

what it means

The Fair Youth, like everything that grows, will find a moment of great perfection and then wither and die. Never to be outdone by death, Shakespeare posits that his friend will be immortal in his verse, even as he gets old and ugly and dies.

fact

Over 500 words in the English language can be attributed to Shakespeare. While it's hard to determine a word's origin, scholars believe that words like "flowery," "madcap," and "courtship" sprang from his writing.

Sonnet 16

But wherefore do not you a mightier way
Make war upon this bloody tyrant, Time?
And fortify your self in your decay
With means more blessed than my barren rhyme?
Now stand you on the top of happy hours,
And many maiden gardens, yet unset,
With virtuous wish would bear you living flowers,
Much liker than your painted counterfeit:
So should the lines of life that life repair,
Which this, Time's pencil, or my pupil pen,
Neither in inward worth nor outward fair,
Can make you live your self in eyes of men.
　　To give away yourself, keeps yourself still,
　　And you must live, drawn by your own sweet skill.

what it means

Still, like any artist Shakespeare has his doubts
about the longevity of his writing. And, once
more, he suggests that the youth fight
death with babies. Because death's
primary goal is to take away
everything lovely.

fact

While some have argued that
Shakespeare is not the actual author of
his works, reliable historical evidence
confirms his authorship. These include
specific references to him and his works
by contemporaries in correspondence
and other documents.

Sonnet 17

Who will believe my verse in time to come,
If it were filled with your most high deserts?
Though yet heaven knows it is but as a tomb
Which hides your life, and shows not half your parts.
If I could write the beauty of your eyes,
And in fresh numbers number all your graces,
The age to come would say 'This poet lies;
Such heavenly touches ne'er touched earthly faces.'
So should my papers, yellowed with their age,
Be scorned, like old men of less truth than tongue,
And your true rights be termed a poet's rage
And stretched metre of an antique song:
But were some child of yours alive that time,
You should live twice, in it, and in my rhyme.

what it means

Shakespeare ends the procreation sequence by
suggesting that the youth must bear children
so that their beauty will prove how great
his sonnets were at capturing their
father's beauty. And, as a bonus,
he'll live in both his children
and in poetry!

fact

Ben Jonson, a contemporary of
Shakespeare's and possible rival,
wrote in an elegy to the Bard that
his writing was such that "neither
man nor muse can praise too much."
Jonson's elegy proclaimed him a natural
genius despite his common upbringing
and simple education.

Sonnet 34

Why didst thou promise such a beauteous day,
And make me travel forth without my cloak,
To let base clouds o'ertake me in my way,
Hiding thy bravery in their rotten smoke?
'Tis not enough that through the cloud thou break,
To dry the rain on my storm-beaten face,
For no man well of such a salve can speak,
That heals the wound, and cures not the disgrace:
Nor can thy shame give physic to my grief;
Though thou repent, yet I have still the loss:
The offender's sorrow lends but weak relief
To him that bears the strong offence's cross.
   Ah! but those tears are pearl which thy love sheds,
   And they are rich and ransom all ill deeds.

what it means

Sonnet 34 reflects on the youth's rejection
of Shakespeare. Despite saying he was
committed in love and friendship, the
youth has fallen through on his
promise that he was a reliable
companion.

fact

Shakespeare possibly died on his
52nd birthday, according to his
baptism and death records.

Sonnet 44

If the dull substance of my flesh were thought,
Injurious distance should not stop my way;
For then despite of space I would be brought,
From limits far remote, where thou dost stay.
No matter then although my foot did stand
Upon the farthest earth removed from thee;
For nimble thought can jump both sea and land
As soon as think the place where he would be.
But ah! thought kills me that I am not thought,
To leap large lengths of miles when thou art gone,
But that, so much of earth and water wrought,
I must attend time's leisure with my moan,
Receiving nought by elements so slow
But heavy tears, badges of either's woe.

what it means

Here, the Bard laments that he cannot merely think of his beloved and suddenly be there. Like many who are away from their loved ones, Shakespeare can only cry "heavy tears."

fact

Shakespeare was buried in Holy Trinity Church in Stratford. In his epitaph, he put a curse on any grave robbers who might have wanted to stop by. His grave remains undisturbed to this day.

Sonnet 50

How heavy do I journey on the way,
When what I seek, my weary travel's end,
Doth teach that ease and that repose to say,
'Thus far the miles are measured from thy friend!'
The beast that bears me, tired with my woe,
Plods dully on, to bear that weight in me,
As if by some instinct the wretch did know
His rider lov'd not speed being made from thee.
The bloody spur cannot provoke him on,
That sometimes anger thrusts into his hide,
Which heavily he answers with a groan,
More sharp to me than spurring to his side;
   For that same groan doth put this in my mind,
   My grief lies onward, and my joy behind.

what it means

The theme of separation continues in this sonnet, as Shakespeare has to leave his beloved for a long journey. He describes his horse as being similarly disinterested in pursuing the journey and carrying his sorrowful weight on his back.

fact

Shakespeare put the curse on his epitaph because digging up graves was very common in his time. Either for robbery, research or making room for more bodies, graves were often disturbed. His fear of this is found in 16 of his plays.

Sonnet 52

So am I as the rich whose blessèd key
Can bring him to his sweet up-lockèd treasure,
The which he will not every hour survey,
For blunting the fine point of seldom pleasure.
Therefore are feasts so solemn and so rare,
Since seldom coming in the long year set,
Like stones of worth they thinly placèd are,
Or captain jewels in the carcanet.
So is the time that keeps you as my chest,
Or as the wardrobe which the robe doth hide,
To make some special instant special blest
By new unfolding his imprisoned pride.
Blessèd are you whose worthiness gives scope,
Being had, to triumph; being lacked, to hope.

what it means

The lover (maybe Shakespeare) now compares himself to the kind of miserly person who wants to hoard a treasure. But he cannot hoard his friend's presence, which, like a prize jewel, is rarely found. He acknowledges he is both pleased and forlorn by the Fair Youth's demeanor.

fact

Shakespeare wrote 37 plays and 154 sonnets, which amounts to about 1 ½ plays per year. He also ran an acting company and a theatre at the same time.

Sonnet 58

That god forbid, that made me first your slave,
I should in thought control your times of pleasure,
Or at your hand th' account of hours to crave,
Being your vassal bound to stay your leisure.
O let me suffer, being at your beck,
Th' imprisoned absence of your liberty;
And patience tame to sufferance bide each check,
Without accusing you of injury.
Be where you list, your charter is so strong
That you yourself may privilege your time
To what you will; to you it doth belong
Yourself to pardon of self-doing crime.
　　I am to wait, though waiting so be hell,
　　Not blame your pleasure, be it ill or well.

what it means

Here, the poet is waiting painfully for just a bit
of the youth's attention. And like a neglected
friend or lover, he does not want to place
demands on the youth's freedom, but
he feels painfully subjected and
ignored because of it.

fact

The Bard was also an actor and
performed in many of his own plays,
as well as those written by others.

" *Thus do I pine and surfeit day by day,
Or gluttoning on all, or all away.* "

Sonnet 75

So are you to my thoughts as food to life,
Or as sweet-season'd showers are to the ground;
And for the peace of you I hold such strife
As 'twixt a miser and his wealth is found.
Now proud as an enjoyer, and anon
Doubting the filching age will steal his treasure;
Now counting best to be with you alone,
Then better'd that the world may see my pleasure:
Sometime all full with feasting on your sight,
And by and by clean starved for a look;
Possessing or pursuing no delight
Save what is had, or must from you be took.
 Thus do I pine and surfeit day by day,
 Or gluttoning on all, or all away.

what it means

Shakespeare here writes of feeling the frantic, unquenchable desire to have the youth within his sight at all times. He is always either starved for his company or delighting in it. Again calling himself a miser, he describes that possessiveness that sometimes comes with infatuation.

Sonnet 77

Thy glass will show thee how thy beauties wear,
Thy dial how thy precious minutes waste;
The vacant leaves thy mind's imprint will bear,
And of this book, this learning mayst thou taste.
The wrinkles which thy glass will truly show
Of mouthed graves will give thee memory;
Thou by thy dial's shady stealth mayst know
Time's thievish progress to eternity.
Look what thy memory cannot contain,
Commit to these waste blanks, and thou shalt find
Those children nursed, delivered from thy brain,
To take a new acquaintance of thy mind.
These offices, so oft as thou wilt look,
Shall profit thee and much enrich thy book.

what it means

Shakespeare encourages his friend to record his thoughts on paper (possibly in a gifted notebook) to improve himself and learn from his mistakes. Since watches and mirrors will remind him of death's approach, it is wise to take time to reflect and grow before that time comes.

fact

It was common for writers to collaborate on plays in the Elizabethan era. The number of works that Shakespeare collaborated on is debated. However, it is known that **The Two Noble Kinsmen**, for example, was attributable to both Shakespeare and playwright John Fletcher.

Sonnet 82

I grant thou wert not married to my Muse,
And therefore mayst without attaint o'erlook
The dedicated words which writers use
Of their fair subject, blessing every book.
Thou art as fair in knowledge as in hue,
Finding thy worth a limit past my praise;
And therefore art enforced to seek anew
Some fresher stamp of the time-bettering days.
And do so, love; yet when they have devised,
What strained touches rhetoric can lend,
Thou truly fair, wert truly sympathized
In true plain words, by thy true-telling friend;
    And their gross painting might be better used
    Where cheeks need blood; in thee it is abused.

what it means

The poet encourages the youth to ignore his rivals, who are not as talented and sincere, in his opinion. He feels that the flattering writing of the "Rival Poets" will corrupt the youth's ego, and that he is instead best served by Shakespeare's honest pen.

fact

Shakespeare is typically called an Elizabethan playwright, but he straddled the Jacobean era as well, as he lived and wrote past the death of Queen Elizabeth I in 1603.

Sonnet 95

How sweet and lovely dost thou make the shame
Which, like a canker in the fragrant rose,
Doth spot the beauty of thy budding name!
O! in what sweets dost thou thy sins enclose.
That tongue that tells the story of thy days,
Making lascivious comments on thy sport,
Cannot dispraise, but in a kind of praise;
Naming thy name blesses an ill report.
O! what a mansion have those vices got
Which for their habitation chose out thee,
Where beauty's veil doth cover every blot
And all things turns to fair that eyes can see!
Take heed, dear heart, of this large privilege;
The hardest knife ill-used doth lose his edge.

what it means

The poet here admonishes the youth for becoming a "mansion" for vice to inhabit, where his beauty covers up his ill deeds. And like any loving friend, he reminds him of his good qualities, while noting that he has a few skeletons in the closet.

fact

The Bard's characters committed suicide 13 times in his plays, with the most famous examples in *Romeo and Juliet* and *Julius Caesar*. This would be a spoiler alert, but these plays were written 400 years ago.

Sonnet 111

O! for my sake do you with Fortune chide,
The guilty goddess of my harmful deeds,
That did not better for my life provide
Than public means which public manners breeds.
Thence comes it that my name receives a brand,
And almost thence my nature is subdued
To what it works in, like the dyer's hand:
Pity me, then, and wish I were renewed;
Whilst, like a willing patient, I will drink
Potions of eisel 'gainst my strong infection;
No bitterness that I will bitter think,
Nor double penance, to correct correction.
   Pity me then, dear friend, and I assure ye,
   Even that your pity is enough to cure me.

what it means

Like any two friends who come from different walks of life, Shakespeare is forced to respond to the youth for his bad habits. As a common person who must gain public attention for his art, he has had to intermingle with common, immoral people.

fact

Shakespeare's religion has been another subject of debate. Legal documents suggest both he and his family were publicly members of the accepted Anglican Church. Based on his work and analysis of historical records, some suggest he may have been secretly Catholic.

" To keep an adjunct to remember thee
Were to import forgetfulness in me. "

Sonnet 122

Thy gift, thy tables, are within my brain
Full charactered with lasting memory,
Which shall above that idle rank remain,
Beyond all date, even to eternity:
Or, at the least, so long as brain and heart
Have faculty by nature to subsist;
Till each to razed oblivion yield his part
Of thee, thy record never can be missed.
That poor retention could not so much hold,
Nor need I tallies thy dear love to score;
Therefore to give them from me was I bold,
To trust those tables that receive thee more:
    To keep an adjunct to remember thee
    Were to import forgetfulness in me.

what it means

In a possibly autobiographical turn, Shakespeare has given away a notebook
given to him by the youth. But, he says, he has already filled his mind with
many thoughts of him that will last much longer in his memory than in a
flimsy book.

Love

Sonnet 10

For shame deny that thou bear'st love to any,
Who for thy self art so unprovident.
Grant, if thou wilt, thou art beloved of many,
But that thou none lov'st is most evident:
For thou art so possessed with murderous hate,
That 'gainst thy self thou stick'st not to conspire,
Seeking that beauteous roof to ruinate
Which to repair should be thy chief desire.
O! change thy thought, that I may change my mind:
Shall hate be fairer lodged than gentle love?
Be, as thy presence is, gracious and kind,
Or to thyself at least kind-hearted prove:
Make thee another self for love of me,
That beauty still may live in thine or thee.

what it means

This sonnet is among the first where the poet takes a personal interest in the youth. He begs that the youth change his selfish demeanor so that the poet will change his opinion of him. The poet's love is half-implied as he asks the youth to make children for his sake.

fact

Scholars believe that some of Shakespeare's plays have been lost to history. *Cardenio* is known to have been performed in 1613, but no copies of it exist. It is believed to be partially adapted from *Don Quixote* and possibly another collaboration with John Fletcher.

Sonnet 62

Sin of self-love possesseth all mine eye
And all my soul, and all my every part;
And for this sin there is no remedy,
It is so grounded inward in my heart.
Methinks no face so gracious is as mine,
No shape so true, no truth of such account;
And for myself mine own worth do define,
As I all other in all worths surmount.
But when my glass shows me myself indeed
Beated and chopp'd with tanned antiquity,
Mine own self-love quite contrary I read;
Self so self-loving were iniquity.
　'Tis thee, myself, that for myself I praise,
　Painting my age with beauty of thy days

what it means

The poet has been accused of being self-involved, possibly by
the youth. He says that self-love is deeply rooted in his heart
as he holds himself in high esteem. But, when looking
at his old and beaten face, he comes to an opposite
conclusion. He is simply praising the youth's
presence in his life, and ornamenting
himself with the youth.

fact

Puritans hated the theater
and the immoral socializing it
attracted. In 1642, at the start
of the English Civil War they
banned theater performances
in London and tore down the
famous Globe Theater (of which
Shakespeare was a shareholder) to
make room for tenements.

66 But since she prick'd thee out for women's pleasure,
Mine be thy love and thy love's use their treasure. 99

Sonnet 20

A woman's face with nature's own hand painted,
Hast thou, the master mistress of my passion;
A woman's gentle heart, but not acquainted
With shifting change, as is false women's fashion:
An eye more bright than theirs, less false in rolling,
Gilding the object whereupon it gazeth;
A man in hue all hues in his controlling,
Which steals men's eyes and women's souls amazeth.
And for a woman wert thou first created;
Till Nature, as she wrought thee, fell a-doting,
And by addition me of thee defeated,
By adding one thing to my purpose nothing.
    But since she prick'd thee out for women's pleasure,
    Mine be thy love and thy love's use their treasure.

what it means

The poet here praises the youth's beauty and brilliance, comparing it to the
false beauty and manner of women. But, as the youth has been "prick'd out for
women's pleasure," Shakespeare asks the poet to be his non-physical love.

Sonnet 21

So is it not with me as with that Muse,
Stirred by a painted beauty to his verse,
Who heaven itself for ornament doth use
And every fair with his fair doth rehearse,
Making a couplement of proud compare
With sun and moon, with earth and sea's rich gems,
With April's first-born flowers, and all things rare,
That heaven's air in this huge rondure hems.
O! let me, true in love, but truly write,
And then believe me, my love is as fair
As any mother's child, though not so bright
As those gold candles fixed in heaven's air:
Let them say more that like of hearsay well;
I will not praise that purpose not to sell.

what it means

Typically, sonneteers compared their loves with everything
fair and beautiful. But here, Shakespeare says he
prefers to be truthful, rather than force comparisons
with suns and moons. It is enough, in his
opinion, to say that the youth is beauty
beyond compare.

fact

Shakespeare's primary
profession was not writing,
but acting and business.

Sonnet 22

My glass shall not persuade me I am old,
So long as youth and thou are of one date;
But when in thee time's furrows I behold,
Then look I death my days should expiate.
For all that beauty that doth cover thee,
Is but the seemly raiment of my heart,
Which in thy breast doth live, as thine in me:
How can I then be elder than thou art?
O! therefore, love, be of thyself so wary
As I, not for myself, but for thee will;
Bearing thy heart, which I will keep so chary
As tender nurse her babe from faring ill.
    Presume not on thy heart when mine is slain,
    Thou gav'st me thine not to give back again.

what it means

The poet contemplates how he and his love will be
intertwined until their deaths. Though he is older, the
poet is made young because he and the youth
share their hearts. Until he dies, the poet says,
he will take care of the youth's heart as
though it were his own.

fact

In 1890, bird fanatic and
Shakespeare lover Eugene
Schieffelin decided to introduce
all of the birds in Shakespeare's
plays to North America. The
most successful of these birds
was the starling—he released
100 starlings that have grown to a
population of 200 million today.

Sonnet 23

As an unperfect actor on the stage,
Who with his fear is put beside his part,
Or some fierce thing replete with too much rage,
Whose strength's abundance weakens his own heart;
So I, for fear of trust, forget to say
The perfect ceremony of love's rite,
And in mine own love's strength seem to decay,
O'ercharged with burthen of mine own love's might.
O! let my looks be then the eloquence
And dumb presagers of my speaking breast,
Who plead for love, and look for recompense,
More than that tongue that more hath more express'd.
O! learn to read what silent love hath writ:
To hear with eyes belongs to love's fine wit.

what it means

Like many lovers, the poet describes why he is tongue-tied
in his love's presence. He likens himself to an actor
with stage fright, forgetting the lines he owes to his
beloved. But, he says, let his looks be the loving
words he cannot say.

fact

Estimates of Shakespeare's
written vocabulary far
outnumber even today's
educated English-speaker—
around 17,000 words.

Sonnet 33

Full many a glorious morning have I seen
Flatter the mountain tops with sovereign eye,
Kissing with golden face the meadows green,
Gilding pale streams with heavenly alchemy;
Anon permit the basest clouds to ride
With ugly rack on his celestial face,
And from the forlorn world his visage hide,
Stealing unseen to west with this disgrace:
Even so my sun one early morn did shine,
With all triumphant splendour on my brow;
But out, alack, he was but one hour mine,
The region cloud hath mask'd him from me now.
    Yet him for this my love no whit disdaineth;
    Suns of the world may stain when heaven's sun staineth.

what it means

The poet and his love have a period of estrangement that results in this famous sonnet, where the youth is described as a sun whose face has turned from his beloved. He was the poet's for only an hour, and now he has hidden. But, as he is golden like the sun, he can hide all he wants.

fact

Ale, a type of beer, was the most popular drink in Shakespeare's time. Wine was much more expensive, so it was not enjoyed frequently except in the upper classes.

Sonnet 25

Let those who are in favour with their stars
Of public honour and proud titles boast,
Whilst I, whom fortune of such triumph bars
Unlook'd for joy in that I honour most.
Great princes' favourites their fair leaves spread
But as the marigold at the sun's eye,
And in themselves their pride lies buried,
For at a frown they in their glory die.
The painful warrior famoused for fight,
After a thousand victories once foiled,
Is from the book of honour razed quite,
And all the rest forgot for which he toiled:
Then happy I, that love and am beloved,
Where I may not remove nor be removed.

what it means

Shakespeare here reflects on the fickleness of success—
money, power and public favor can disappear
without warning. But he and his love, sitting on
the thrones of each other's hearts, cannot
lose their good fortune.

fact

Shakespeare's sister, Anne,
died at age 8 from the Black
Death, also known as the
bubonic plague. Shakespeare
was lucky to have survived
the extremely contagious and
deadly disease.

Sonnet 26

Lord of my love, to whom in vassalage
Thy merit hath my duty strongly knit,
To thee I send this written embassage,
To witness duty, not to show my wit:
Duty so great, which wit so poor as mine
May make seem bare, in wanting words to show it,
But that I hope some good conceit of thine
In thy soul's thought, all naked, will bestow it:
Till whatsoever star that guides my moving,
Points on me graciously with fair aspect,
And puts apparel on my tottered loving,
To show me worthy of thy sweet respect:
　　Then may I dare to boast how I do love thee;
　　Till then, not show my head where thou mayst prove me.

what it means

Shakespeare tells the youth to view his sonnet as a testament to his
loyalty, not as a showy attempt to seem witty. He hopes that he
will be inspired to dress up his loyalty with beautiful words
so that he will prove worthy of the youth's love. The
message is tongue-in-cheek, however, as the
mere existence of the sonnet shows that
Shakespeare is quite confident in his wit.

fact

Families were large in
Shakespeare's time since
the child mortality rate was
high. Shakespeare had seven
siblings, three of whom died
at a young age.

Sonnet 27

Weary with toil, I haste me to my bed,
The dear repose for limbs with travel tired;
But then begins a journey in my head
To work my mind, when body's work's expired:
For then my thoughts--from far where I abide--
Intend a zealous pilgrimage to thee,
And keep my drooping eyelids open wide,
Looking on darkness which the blind do see:
Save that my soul's imaginary sight
Presents thy shadow to my sightless view,
Which, like a jewel hung in ghastly night,
Makes black night beauteous, and her old face new.
Lo! thus, by day my limbs, by night my mind,
For thee, and for myself, no quiet find.

what it means

Shakespeare here seems to suffer from sleeplessness
brought on by his infatuation with the youth. In the
day, he cannot stop thinking of his love, and at
night, his mind wanders vast distances to be
with him. And while the youth's image
makes the ghastly night beautiful, he
can find no rest.

fact

Shakespeare lived most of
his adult life in London, but
returned to Stratford-upon-
Avon to live with his wife and
daughters in the last few years
of his life.

Sonnet 31

Thy bosom is endeared with all hearts,
Which I by lacking have supposed dead;
And there reigns Love, and all Love's loving parts,
And all those friends which I thought buried.
How many a holy and obsequious tear
Hath dear religious love stol'n from mine eye,
As interest of the dead, which now appear
But things removed that hidden in thee lie!
Thou art the grave where buried love doth live,
Hung with the trophies of my lovers gone,
Who all their parts of me to thee did give,
That due of many now is thine alone:
    Their images I loved, I view in thee,
    And thou (all they) hast all the all of me.

what it means

The poet's beloved here is the center of all his love—past loves and friends forgotten find new life in his image. The love he thought was lost is renewed in their affection. Though they are only mementos of the past, the feelings are brought alive and directed at the youth.

fact

Shakespeare's father, John, was a glove-maker who held a few public service positions in Stratford, including the borough's official "ale taster."

Sonnet 35

No more be grieved atthat which thou hast done:
Roses have thorns, and silver fountains mud:
Clouds and eclipses stain both moon and sun,
And loathsome canker lives in sweetest bud.
All men make faults, and even I in this,
Authorizing thy trespass with compare,
Myself corrupting, salving thy amiss,
Excusing thy sins more than thy sins are;
For to thy sensual fault I bring in sense,
Thy adverse party is thy advocate,
And 'gainst myself a lawful plea commence:
Such civil war is in my love and hate,
That I an accessary needs must be,
To that sweet thief which sourly robs from me.

what it means

Here the poet both defends and grieves the sins of his lover,
possibly related to philandering and unfaithfulness. He
notes that all beautiful things have a bad side—roses
have thorns. He laments how he is drawn into
the youth's sin because of his love for him.

fact

Shakespeare created the
sonnets whenever London's
theaters were closed because
of the plague or other reasons.
In the meantime, he was paid
by wealthy patrons to write
the sonnets.

Sonnet 36

Let me confess that we two must be twain,
Although our undivided loves are one:
So shall those blots that do with me remain,
Without thy help, by me be borne alone.
In our two loves there is but one respect,
Though in our lives a separable spite,
Which though it alter not love's sole effect,
Yet doth it steal sweet hours from love's delight.
I may not evermore acknowledge thee,
Lest my bewailed guilt should do thee shame,
Nor thou with public kindness honour me,
Unless thou take that honour from thy name:
But do not so, I love thee in such sort,
As thou being mine, mine is thy good report.

what it means

In another one of the separation sonnets, the poet tells the
youth that they must part ways for a time because of
their transgressions. Though they will separate, it
is because they are united in love and must
maintain both of their reputations.

fact

Shakespeare's sonnets were
printed in 1609, possibly
without his permission. The
publisher, Thomas Thorpe, may
have obtained the copies by
theft or other means. Without
him, however, they may never
have been printed.

Sonnet 39

O! how thy worth with manners may I sing,
When thou art all the better part of me?
What can mine own praise to mine own self bring?
And what is't but mine own when I praise thee?
Even for this, let us divided live,
And our dear love lose name of single one,
That by this separation I may give
That due to thee which thou deserv'st alone.
O absence! what a torment wouldst thou prove,
Were it not thy sour leisure gave sweet leave,
To entertain the time with thoughts of love,
Which time and thoughts so sweetly doth deceive,
And that thou teachest how to make one twain,
By praising him here who doth hence remain.

what it means

The poet here contemplates the benefits of being apart
from his love. Having grown too intertwined in their
identities, he finds that by praising his friend in his
poetry he is only praising himself. By separating,
he will fill lonely hours with learning to love
the youth properly again.

fact

Until he became wealthy, it's
likely that Shakespeare made a
six-day walk between Stratford-
upon-Avon and London to
commute between his home
and his work. After that, he
might have travelled by horse.

Sonnet 40

Take all my loves, my love, yea take them all;
What hast thou then more than thou hadst before?
No love, my love, that thou mayst true love call;
All mine was thine, before thou hadst this more.
Then, if for my love, thou my love receivest,
I cannot blame thee, for my love thou usest;
But yet be blam'd, if thou thy self deceivest
By wilful taste of what thyself refusest.
I do forgive thy robbery, gentle thief,
Although thou steal thee all my poverty:
And yet, love knows it is a greater grief
To bear love's wrong, than hate's known injury.
   Lascivious grace, in whom all ill well shows,
   Kill me with spites yet we must not be foes.

what it means

In this sonnet, the poet wonders what motive the youth
has to steal his mistress. By telling him to take all his
loves, he aims to give the youth what he wants, so
that their love will remain after the betrayal.
Still, the confused feelings following his
wanton deception linger.

fact

In Shakespeare's youth,
school days were 11 or
12 hours long, Monday to
Saturday, with a two-hour
break for dinner.

Sonnet 41

Those pretty wrongs that liberty commits,
When I am sometime absent from thy heart,
Thy beauty, and thy years full well befits,
For still temptation follows where thou art.
Gentle thou art, and therefore to be won,
Beauteous thou art, therefore to be assailed;
And when a woman woos, what woman's son
Will sourly leave her till he have prevailed?
Ay me! but yet thou mightst my seat forbear,
And chide thy beauty and thy straying youth,
Who lead thee in their riot even there
Where thou art forced to break a twofold truth:
Hers by thy beauty tempting her to thee,
Thine by thy beauty being false to me.

what it means

Here Shakespeare tries to reason out the youth's motives,
deciding that his infidelities stem from his age, beauty
and temptation. Being a nobleman, women desire
him, and what man could refuse that? But,
he asks, couldn't he resist breaking his
friendship by stealing his mistress?

fact

There would have been no
real "teenager" period in
Shakespeare's life. In the 16th
and 17th centuries, children
were seen as miniature adults
to be pushed into adulthood as
soon as possible. In **Romeo and
Juliet**, Juliet is just 14 when her
parents arrange her marriage.

Sonnet 42

That thou hast her it is not all my grief,
And yet it may be said I loved her dearly;
That she hath thee is of my wailing chief,
A loss in love that touches me more nearly.
Loving offenders thus I will excuse ye:
Thou dost love her, because thou know'st I love her;
And for my sake even so doth she abuse me,
Suffering my friend for my sake to approve her.
If I lose thee, my loss is my love's gain,
And losing her, my friend hath found that loss;
Both find each other, and I lose both twain,
And both for my sake lay on me this cross:
    But here's the joy; my friend and I are one;
    Sweet flattery! then she loves but me alone.

what it means

The poet continues reproving his friend for having taken his mistress, and his loss of both his loves—his friend and his romantic partner. He rationalizes the pain by saying that the love they share comes from his love for both of them. But, if he and the youth are one, then the mistress loves only him.

fact

Shakespeare's wife, Anne Hathaway, was 26 and three months pregnant when 18-year-old Shakespeare married her. Even at 17, Shakespeare was getting himself into trouble.

66 This told, I joy; but then no longer glad,
I send them back again and straight grow sad. 99

Sonnet 45

The other two, slight air and purging fire,
Are both with thee, wherever I abide;
The first my thought, the other my desire,
These present-absent with swift motion slide.
For when these quicker elements are gone
In tender embassy of love to thee,
My life, being made of four, with two alone
Sinks down to death, oppressed with melancholy;
Until life's composition be recured
By those swift messengers return'd from thee,
Who even but now come back again, assured
Of thy fair health, recounting it to me:
    This told, I joy; but then no longer glad,
    I send them back again and straight grow sad.

what it means

Shakespeare finds that his desire and thoughts—referred to as fire and air here—remain with the youth, wherever he is. When they are apart he is missing these vital parts of himself, leading him into melancholy.

Sonnet 47

Betwixt mine eye and heart a league is took,
And each doth good turns now unto the other:
When that mine eye is famish'd for a look,
Or heart in love with sighs himself doth smother,
With my love's picture then my eye doth feast,
And to the painted banquet bids my heart;
Another time mine eye is my heart's guest,
And in his thoughts of love doth share a part:
So, either by thy picture or my love,
Thy self away, art present still with me;
For thou not farther than my thoughts canst move,
And I am still with them, and they with thee;
Or, if they sleep, thy picture in my sight
Awakes my heart, to heart's and eyes' delight.

what it means

Shakespeare discusses elsewhere the struggle between eye and heart, but here they work in tandem. This is another sonnet of absence, but it is not a painful one. His eyes can remember the youth in sleep, and his heart continues to love him. Therefore, his thoughts are always with the youth.

fact

Shakespeare, like most people of the time, probably only bathed once every few weeks or months (depending how rich he was). Running water didn't exist and clean water was hard to come by.

Sonnet 48

How careful was I when I took my way,
Each trifle under truest bars to thrust,
That to my use it might unused stay
From hands of falsehood, in sure wards of trust!
But thou, to whom my jewels trifles are,
Most worthy comfort, now my greatest grief,
Thou best of dearest, and mine only care,
Art left the prey of every vulgar thief.
Thee have I not locked up in any chest,
Save where thou art not, though I feel thou art,
Within the gentle closure of my breast,
From whence at pleasure thou mayst come and part;
   And even thence thou wilt be stol'n I fear,
   For truth proves thievish for a prize so dear.

what it means

Shakespeare laments that he cannot lock up his love as he
can any other possession. His love, then, has become a
source of worry and sadness. Though he is in the
poet's heart, he can leave or be stolen at any
time and hurt him.

fact

Scholars aren't sure how
Shakespeare started his career
in his early 20s. In 1592
documents begin to list him as
an actor and playwright, but
it's uncertain what his work or
writing was like before then.

Sonnet 51

Thus can my love excuse the slow offence
Of my dull bearer when from thee I speed:
From where thou art why should I haste me thence?
Till I return, of posting is no need.
O! what excuse will my poor beast then find,
When swift extremity can seem but slow?
Then should I spur, though mounted on the wind,
In winged speed no motion shall I know,
Then can no horse with my desire keep pace.
Therefore desire, (of perfect'st love being made)
Shall neigh, no dull flesh, in his fiery race;
But love, for love, thus shall excuse my jade-
Since from thee going, he went wilful-slow,
Towards thee I'll run, and give him leave to go.

what it means

The poet is taking another journey on horseback, but here
his desires are more desperate. Though his horse may
be running, as long as he is away from the youth he
will feel as though they are standing still. When
he returns, he will race back, pushing his
desire to its limit.

fact

Shakespeare supposedly
played unassuming actor
roles to give him time to
write. He even may have
played the ghost in *Hamlet*
for a time.

Sonnet 56

Sweet love, renew thy force; be it not said
Thy edge should blunter be than appetite,
Which but to-day by feeding is allayed,
To-morrow sharpened in his former might:
So, love, be thou, although to-day thou fill
Thy hungry eyes, even till they wink with fulness,
To-morrow see again, and do not kill
The spirit of love, with a perpetual dulness.
Let this sad interim like the ocean be
Which parts the shore, where two contracted new
Come daily to the banks, that when they see
Return of love, more blest may be the view;
　　As call it winter, which being full of care,
　　Makes summer's welcome, thrice more wished, more rare.

what it means

The poet encourages his love to stay strong despite their separation. Although some say love is weaker than lust, he reassures him this is untrue. He tells the youth not to dull his affection in this time, and to think of it as a long winter before a lovely summer.

fact

A playwright in Shakespeare's early years named Robert Greene insulted him in a pamphlet, writing that he was an "upstart Crow." Many disdained Shakespeare's lack of a university education despite his writing ability.

Sonnet 57

Being your slave what should I do but tend
Upon the hours, and times of your desire?
I have no precious time at all to spend;
Nor services to do, till you require.
Nor dare I chide the world without end hour,
Whilst I, my sovereign, watch the clock for you,
Nor think the bitterness of absence sour,
When you have bid your servant once adieu;
Nor dare I question with my jealous thought
Where you may be, or your affairs suppose,
But, like a sad slave, stay and think of nought
Save, where you are, how happy you make those.
So true a fool is love, that in your will,
Though you do anything, he thinks no ill.

what it means

The poet tells the youth he is waiting patiently for him despite
jealousy and anxiety about what he's doing, and that he
feels like a slave in doing so. But, ironically, the mere
mention of these things betrays his supposed
patience. He calls himself a faithful fool for
the youth's absent affections.

fact

In Shakespeare's time, theaters
were partly outdoors and had
no curtains and little scenery.
But these limitations worked
well with Shakespeare's
writing, as audiences had to
pay close attention to his words
and their meaning.

Sonnet 61

Is it thy will, thy image should keep open
My heavy eyelids to the weary night?
Dost thou desire my slumbers should be broken,
While shadows like to thee do mock my sight?
Is it thy spirit that thou send'st from thee
So far from home into my deeds to pry,
To find out shames and idle hours in me,
The scope and tenor of thy jealousy?
O, no! thy love, though much, is not so great:
It is my love that keeps mine eye awake:
Mine own true love that doth my rest defeat,
To play the watchman ever for thy sake:
  For thee watch I, whilst thou dost wake elsewhere,
  From me far off, with others all too near.

what it means

The poet's dissatisfaction continues as he lies awake,
feeling foolish for his love of the youth. His beloved
appears to be elsewhere, possibly philandering
with the poet's mistress.

fact

Theatergoers could buy
snacks, like fruit, to eat during
the performance. The audience
often threw food at the players
when they were dissatisfied
with the performance.

" *Thus have I had thee, as a dream doth flatter,
In sleep a king, but waking no such matter.* "

Sonnet 87

Farewell! thou art too dear for my possessing,
And like enough thou know'st thy estimate,
The charter of thy worth gives thee releasing;
My bonds in thee are all determinate.
For how do I hold thee but by thy granting?
And for that riches where is my deserving?
The cause of this fair gift in me is wanting,
And so my patent back again is swerving.
Thy self thou gavest, thy own worth then not knowing,
Or me to whom thou gav'st it else mistaking;
So thy great gift, upon misprision growing,
Comes home again, on better judgement making.
  Thus have I had thee, as a dream doth flatter,
  In sleep a king, but waking no such matter.

what it means

The poet here has been finally rejected by the youth, and he bids him farewell from the start. And though the poet comments again that he cannot place a hold on his friend, his use of legal and financial language indicates that he may think the rejection was a cynical social decision.

Sonnet 88

When thou shalt be disposed to set me light,
And place my merit in the eye of scorn,
Upon thy side, against myself I'll fight,
And prove thee virtuous, though thou art forsworn.
With mine own weakness being best acquainted,
Upon thy part I can set down a story
Of faults concealed, wherein I am attainted;
That thou in losing me shalt win much glory:
And I by this will be a gainer too;
For bending all my loving thoughts on thee,
The injuries that to myself I do,
Doing thee vantage, double-vantage me.
Such is my love, to thee I so belong,
That for thy right, myself will bear all wrong.

what it means

Sonnet 88 continues the theme of rejection, where
the youth has begun to speak ill lies of his former
companion. Providing a bit of a guilt trip, the poet
says he loves him so dearly that he'll speak ill
of himself to benefit the youth and make
him seem honest.

fact

Among his many
innovations, Shakespeare
subverted the typical love
sonnet by writing many that
had double meanings, were
self-loathing and bitter, and
even homoerotic.

Sonnet 89

Say that thou didst forsake me for some fault,
And I will comment upon that offence:
Speak of my lameness, and I straight will halt,
Against thy reasons making no defence.
Thou canst not, love, disgrace me half so ill,
To set a form upon desired change,
As I'll myself disgrace; knowing thy will,
I will acquaintance strangle, and look strange;
Be absent from thy walks; and in my tongue
Thy sweet beloved name no more shall dwell,
Lest I, too much profane, should do it wrong,
And haply of our old acquaintance tell.
 For thee, against my self I'll vow debate,
 For I must ne'er love him whom thou dost hate.

what it means

Pushing the previous sentiment even further, Shakespeare
vows to avoid the youth and abide by any lies he tells.
If he says the poet limps, he'll walk with one. If
he does not love the poet, then he won't
love himself either.

fact

Shakespeare invented not
only words, but phrases—
"vanish into thin air," "flesh
and blood," and "be cruel to
be kind" are attributed to him.

Sonnet 90

Then hate me when thou wilt; if ever, now;
Now, while the world is bent my deeds to cross,
Join with the spite of fortune, make me bow,
And do not drop in for an after-loss:
Ah! do not, when my heart hath 'scaped this sorrow,
Come in the rearward of a conquered woe;
Give not a windy night a rainy morrow,
To linger out a purposed overthrow.
If thou wilt leave me, do not leave me last,
When other petty griefs have done their spite,
But in the onset come: so shall I taste
At first the very worst of fortune's might;
And other strains of woe, which now seem woe,
Compared with loss of thee, will not seem so

what it means

The poet finally asks the youth to make sure his
rejection is certain. He doesn't need another
sorrow when luck is currently not in his favor.
Leave me in the beginning, he says, so
that the worst will be done.

fact

The inventory of
Shakespeare's possessions,
an important legal document
kept in London records, was
probably destroyed in the
Great Fire of 1666.

Sonnet 91

Some glory in their birth, some in their skill,
Some in their wealth, some in their body's force,
Some in their garments though new-fangled ill;
Some in their hawks and hounds, some in their horse;
And every humour hath his adjunct pleasure,
Wherein it finds a joy above the rest:
But these particulars are not my measure,
All these I better in one general best.
Thy love is better than high birth to me,
Richer than wealth, prouder than garments' cost,
Of more delight than hawks and horses be;
And having thee, of all men's pride I boast:
    Wretched in this alone, that thou mayst take
    All this away, and me most wretched make.

what it means

The poet describes all the things that bring pride to people,
from frivolous clothing to wealth to high social status. His
beloved is above all these possessions and makes the
poet a happier man for it. But there is a catch—
the love can leave at any time.

fact

Before the First Folio, some
of Shakespeare's plays were
printed as cheap quarto editions
(some were copied from
memory). A few survive today,
though the Folio is the first near-
complete collection of the plays.

Sonnet 93

So shall I live, supposing thou art true,
Like a deceived husband; so love's face
May still seem love to me, though altered new;
Thy looks with me, thy heart in other place:
For there can live no hatred in thine eye,
Therefore in that I cannot know thy change.
In many's looks, the false heart's history
Is writ in moods, and frowns, and wrinkles strange.
But heaven in thy creation did decree
That in thy face sweet love should ever dwell;
Whate'er thy thoughts, or thy heart's workings be,
Thy looks should nothing thence, but sweetness tell.
How like Eve's apple doth thy beauty grow,
If thy sweet virtue answer not thy show!

what it means

Referring to himself as a deceived husband, Shakespeare says
he will assume his love is faithful to him, despite knowing
it is a lie. But, he says, while most people express their
sins in their face or gloomy moods, nature created
the youth to always express sweet love. Like Eve's
apple, he's not as virtuous as he appears.

fact

There are two versions of
King Lear with significantly
different endings, as well as
major speeches that change
the nature of key characters.

Sonnet 98

From you have I been absent in the spring,
When proud pied April, dressed in all his trim,
Hath put a spirit of youth in every thing,
That heavy Saturn laughed and leapt with him.
Yet nor the lays of birds, nor the sweet smell
Of different flowers in odour and in hue,
Could make me any summer's story tell,
Or from their proud lap pluck them where they grew:
Nor did I wonder at the lily's white,
Nor praise the deep vermilion in the rose;
They were but sweet, but figures of delight,
Drawn after you, you pattern of all those.
    Yet seemed it winter still, and you away,
    As with your shadow I with these did play.

what it means

The poet describes a spring when he was away from the
youth, and compares him to all the lovely things the
season brought. But all of the lovely flowers, he
writes, cannot compare to his love. They were
mere imitations, making him feel as though
it were still winter.

fact

Edward de Vere, the 17th Earl
of Oxford, has been proposed
as a leading contender to be the
"real" Shakespeare, but scholars
believe it's unlikely. The Bard is as
well-documented as any historical
figure of the time could have been,
and the Earl would have had little
reason to write under a pseudonym.

66 Finding the first conceit of love there bred
Where time and outward form would show it dead. 99

Sonnet 108

What's in the brain that ink may character
Which hath not figured to thee my true spirit?
What's new to speak, what now to register,
That may express my love or thy dear merit?
Nothing, sweet boy; but yet, like prayers divine,
I must each day say o'er the very same,
Counting no old thing old, thou mine, I thine,
Ev'n as when first I hallowed thy fair name.
So that eternal love in love's fresh case
Weighs not the dust and injury of age,
Nor gives to necessary wrinkles place,
But makes antiquity for aye his page,
Finding the first conceit of love there bred
Where time and outward form would show it dead.

what it means

The youth and the poet have both grown older, and the poet wonders if there is anything more to say of their love. He concludes that it is enough that his love is unaffected by the onslaught of wrinkles and age.

Sonnet 102

My love is strengthened, though more weak in seeming;
I love not less, though less the show appear;
That love is merchandized, whose rich esteeming,
The owner's tongue doth publish every where.
Our love was new, and then but in the spring,
When I was wont to greet it with my lays;
As Philomel in summer's front doth sing,
And stops his pipe in growth of riper days:
Not that the summer is less pleasant now
Than when her mournful hymns did hush the night,
But that wild music burthens every bough,
And sweets grown common lose their dear delight.
Therefore like her, I sometime hold my tongue:
Because I would not dull you with my song.

what it means

After a bit of silence toward his love, the poet explains that
he was merely showing his love less. He loves the youth
just as much, but if he overwhelms him with poems
and declarations it will become less special.

fact

Shakespeare's first poems, **Venus
and Adonis** and **The Rape of
Lucrece**, were published and
dedicated to Henry Wriothesley,
the Earl of Southampton, in
1593 and 1594. Wriothesley is
believed to be the "Fair Youth" of
the sonnets.

Sonnet 104

To me, fair friend, you never can be old,
For as you were when first your eye I ey'd,
Such seems your beauty still. Three winters cold,
Have from the forests shook three summers' pride,
Three beauteous springs to yellow autumn turned,
In process of the seasons have I seen,
Three April perfumes in three hot Junes burned,
Since first I saw you fresh, which yet are green.
Ah! yet doth beauty like a dial-hand,
Steal from his figure, and no pace perceived;
So your sweet hue, which methinks still doth stand,
Hath motion, and mine eye may be deceived:
    For fear of which, hear this thou age unbred:
    Ere you were born was beauty's summer dead.

what it means

In a sweet declaration of love, the poet reassures his love that
he will never grow old in his eyes. But time is passing and
his beauty will fade, even if it hasn't yet. He tells future
generations that when they are born, beauty itself
will have passed long ago with the youth.

fact

Shakespeare found success
quickly after the publication
of his first plays in 1594. By
1597, he had bought New
Place, the largest house in
Stratford-upon-Avon, and moved
his family into it.

Sonnet 109

O! never say that I was false of heart,
Though absence seemed my flame to qualify,
As easy might I from my self depart
As from my soul which in thy breast doth lie:
That is my home of love: if I have ranged,
Like him that travels, I return again;
Just to the time, not with the time exchanged,
So that myself bring water for my stain.
Never believe though in my nature reigned,
All frailties that besiege all kinds of blood,
That it could so preposterously be stained,
To leave for nothing all thy sum of good;
For nothing this wide universe I call,
Save thou, my rose, in it thou art my all.

what it means

The poet tells the youth not to worry if he has left
temporarily. He can't separate himself from his love
with mere distance—they are one. He would never
abandon him for someone else. In all the
universe, he is the poet's everything.

fact

By end of Queen Elizabeth I's
reign, Shakespeare had gained
fame as a poet and playwright
and was called to perform
several of his plays for the
queen and her court.

Sonnet 110

Alas! 'tis true, I have gone here and there,
And made my self a motley to the view,
Gored mine own thoughts, sold cheap what is most dear,
Made old offences of affections new;
Most true it is, that I have looked on truth
Askance and strangely; but, by all above,
These blenches gave my heart another youth,
And worse essays proved thee my best of love.
Now all is done, have what shall have no end:
Mine appetite I never more will grind
On newer proof, to try an older friend,
A god in love, to whom I am confined.
    Then give me welcome, next my heaven the best,
    Even to thy pure and most most loving breast.

what it means

The poet has committed some kind of infidelity, possibly a
reference to his career as an actor and playwright. With
the theaters located near taverns and brothels, there
were plenty of opportunities to act in a way
offensive to the youth. His straying, he says,
has only renewed his love for the youth.

fact

Shakespeare's early plays
were primarily histories and
comedies, such as **Henry VI**,
Titus Andronicus, and
A Midsummer Night's Dream.

Sonnet 112

Your love and pity doth the impression fill,
Which vulgar scandal stamped upon my brow;
For what care I who calls me well or ill,
So you o'er-green my bad, my good allow?
You are my all-the-world, and I must strive
To know my shames and praises from your tongue;
None else to me, nor I to none alive,
That my steeled sense or changes right or wrong.
In so profound abysm I throw all care
Of others' voices, that my adder's sense
To critic and to flatterer stopped are.
Mark how with my neglect I do dispense:
You are so strongly in my purpose bred,
That all the world besides methinks y'are dead.

what it means

Shakespeare has seen some kind of dip in popular opinion,
made up only by the affection and pity of the youth.
Because of him, he writes, the whole world can hold
him in low esteem and it wouldn't matter. Deaf
to criticism or flattery, he has ears only for
what the youth has to say about him.

fact

In London, Shakespeare's
success allowed him to
move to a nicer part of town
by today's Silver Street and
the Barbican Centre in 1602.
He wrote many of his greatest
tragedies, such as *Hamlet* and
King Lear, in that location.

Sonnet 117

Accuse me thus: that I have scanted all,
Wherein I should your great deserts repay,
Forgot upon your dearest love to call,
Whereto all bonds do tie me day by day;
That I have frequent been with unknown minds,
And given to time your own dear-purchased right;
That I have hoisted sail to all the winds
Which should transport me farthest from your sight.
Book both my wilfulness and errors down,
And on just proof surmise accumulate;
Bring me within the level of your frown,
But shoot not at me in your wakened hate;
   Since my appeal says I did strive to prove
   The constancy and virtue of your love.

what it means

Accuse me, writes the poet, of straying, wasting time with stranger, and of forgetting you. He tells the youth to frown, but not hate him. The poet has done all these things to test the constancy of his love.

fact

In Shakespeare's time, women were not allowed to be actors in the theater. Female parts were played by adolescent boys. Women did not appear on London stages until about 50 years after Shakespeare's death.

Time and Death

Sonnet 2

When forty winters shall besiege thy brow,
And dig deep trenches in thy beauty's field,
Thy youth's proud livery so gazed on now,
Will be a totter'd weed of small worth held:
Then being asked, where all thy beauty lies,
    Where all the treasure of thy lusty days;
To say, within thine own deep sunken eyes,
Were an all-eating shame, and thriftless praise.
How much more praise deserv'd thy beauty's use,
    If thou couldst answer 'This fair child of mine
Shall sum my count, and make my old excuse,'
    Proving his beauty by succession thine!
This were to be new made when thou art old,
And see thy blood warm when thou feel'st it cold.

what it means

The poet tells the youth that when he is old, others will ask
where his beauty went, but will not believe him when
they see his withered form. It would be a much
better excuse, he says, if he had a child: both
a symbol of his stressful parenting
and of his beauty.

fact

The first rave review of
Shakespeare's plays was by
writer Francis Meres, who was
a year older than Shakespeare.
His critical account of the Bard's
work has been vital in dating the
creation of his plays.

Sonnet 5

Those hours, that with gentle work did frame
The lovely gaze where every eye doth dwell,
Will play the tyrants to the very same
And that unfair which fairly doth excel;
For never-resting time leads summer on
To hideous winter, and confounds him there;
Sap checked with frost, and lusty leaves quite gone,
Beauty o'er-snowed and bareness every where:
Then were not summer's distillation left,
A liquid prisoner pent in walls of glass,
Beauty's effect with beauty were bereft,
Nor it, nor no remembrance what it was:
　　But flowers distilled, though they with winter meet,
　　Leese but their show; their substance still lives sweet.

what it means

Time, says the Bard, will lead the youth into old age and terrible
winter. He compares the youth to a flower that should be
distilled, with children, into a perfume.

fact

Music was used in Shakespeare's
plays, and typically at least one
song was included in every play.
Only the direst tragedies would
lack music. Plays performed
before a royal court had a
musical ensemble, while those
for the public would have a less
elaborate set-up.

Sonnet 7

Lo! in the orient when the gracious light
Lifts up his burning head, each under eye
Doth homage to his new-appearing sight,
Serving with looks his sacred majesty;
And having climbed the steep-up heavenly hill,
Resembling strong youth in his middle age,
Yet mortal looks adore his beauty still,
Attending on his golden pilgrimage:
But when from highmost pitch, with weary car,
Like feeble age, he reeleth from the day,
The eyes, 'fore duteous, now converted are
From his low tract, and look another way:
So thou, thyself outgoing in thy noon
Unlooked on diest unless thou get a son.

what it means

The sun is adored when its light rises in the east, and
everyone on earth pays homage to it by gazing on its
beauty. Like the sun, the youth has this majestic
beauty, but he is wasting his energies on
women. Without a son, the day will
set on his beauty.

fact

It is very difficult to determine
which songs Shakespeare might
have used in his plays, as very
few of them have survived. More
difficult still is determining the
melodies of these songs.

Sonnet 19

Devouring Time, blunt thou the lion's paws,
And make the earth devour her own sweet brood;
Pluck the keen teeth from the fierce tiger's jaws,
And burn the long-lived phoenix in her blood;
Make glad and sorry seasons as thou fleet'st,
And do whate'er thou wilt, swift-footed Time,
To the wide world and all her fading sweets;
But I forbid thee one most heinous crime:
O! carve not with thy hours my love's fair brow,
Nor draw no lines there with thine antique pen;
Him in thy course untainted do allow
For beauty's pattern to succeeding men.

    Yet, do thy worst old Time: despite thy wrong,
    My love shall in my verse ever live young.

what it means

Shakespeare pleads with time that it not take away his love's
beauty. It can have anything else, he writes, but not
that. Do your worst, he beckons, since his love
will live on in his poetry.

fact

The Bard referred to musical
instruments as double entendre
or metaphor is in his plays. In Act
II, scene 3 of **Cymbeline**, Cloten
makes some rather "penetrating"
comments on his playing ability,
so to speak.

66 *And nothing 'gainst Time's scythe can make defence*
Save breed, to brave him when he takes thee hence. **99**

Sonnet 12

When I do count the clock that tells the time,
And see the brave day sunk in hideous night;
When I behold the violet past prime,
And sable curls, all silvered o'er with white;
When lofty trees I see barren of leaves,
Which erst from heat did canopy the herd,
And summer's green all girded up in sheaves,
Borne on the bier with white and bristly beard,
Then of thy beauty do I question make,
That thou among the wastes of time must go,
Since sweets and beauties do themselves forsake
And die as fast as they see others grow;
    And nothing 'gainst Time's scythe can make defence
    Save breed, to brave him when he takes thee hence.

what it means

The ravages of time take away beauty from all. Curly black hair turns white,
violets wilt, and soon the youth's beauty will fade as well. The only way to
defy time's onslaught, the Bard says, is with children.

Sonnet 29

When in disgrace with fortune and men's eyes
I all alone beweep my outcast state,
And trouble deaf heaven with my bootless cries,
And look upon myself, and curse my fate,
Wishing me like to one more rich in hope,
Featured like him, like him with friends possessed,
Desiring this man's art, and that man's scope,
With what I most enjoy contented least;
Yet in these thoughts my self almost despising,
Haply I think on thee, and then my state,
Like to the lark at break of day arising
From sullen earth, sings hymns at heaven's gate;
For thy sweet love remembered such wealth brings
That then I scorn to change my state with kings.

what it means

When I'm an outcast and envious of others' success and
wealth, writes the poet, only thoughts of my love can
cure me. Like a morning songbird, he sings to
the heavens. He wouldn't trade places with
kings, because he has the wealth of
the youth's love.

fact

Shakespeare used common folk
music in his plays, not the very
complex church music written by
trained composers, like William
Byrd and Thomas Weelkes.
Whether he had disdain for this
upper-class music is uncertain,
but it's likely it would have gone
over the heads of his audience.

Sonnet 49

Against that time, if ever that time come,
When I shall see thee frown on my defects,
When as thy love hath cast his utmost sum,
Called to that audit by advis'd respects;
Against that time when thou shalt strangely pass,
And scarcely greet me with that sun, thine eye,
When love, converted from the thing it was,
Shall reasons find of settled gravity;
Against that time do I ensconce me here,
Within the knowledge of mine own desert,
And this my hand, against my self uprear,
To guard the lawful reasons on thy part:

    To leave poor me thou hast the strength of laws,
    Since why to love I can allege no cause.

what it means

Shakespeare writes of a future time when the youth will frown
at his old age and wrinkles and lose his love for the poet.
In anticipation of it, the poet assures the youth that
he deserves little of his love in the first place: if
he can't justify the youth's love, he can't
blame him for his eventual departure.

fact

Shakespeare's last play was
The Two Noble Kinsmen,
believed to be written around
1613. He would have been
49 at the time, just three years
before his death.

Sonnet 63

Against my love shall be as I am now,
With Time's injurious hand crushed and o'erworn;
When hours have drained his blood and filled his brow
With lines and wrinkles; when his youthful morn
Hath travelled on to age's steepy night;
And all those beauties whereof now he's king
Are vanishing, or vanished out of sight,
Stealing away the treasure of his spring;
For such a time do I now fortify
Against confounding age's cruel knife,
That he shall never cut from memory
My sweet love's beauty, though my lover's life:
His beauty shall in these black lines be seen,
And they shall live, and he in them still green.

what it means

Shakespeare writes that the youth will one day be worn out
by time and moved into old age. To defend himself
against this cruel truth, he keep his memories of
the youth within his poetry. With his beauty
visible in the lines of verse, the poet
will help him survive.

fact

The details of how Shakespeare's
plays were performed—the props,
the way lines were delivered, the
length of performance, entrances
and exits—are somewhat unclear
to modern players. Today, a
theatre director and others oversee
and decide how the play will be
performed.

Sonnet 64

When I have seen by Time's fell hand defaced
The rich proud cost of outworn buried age;
When sometime lofty towers I see down-razed,
And brass eternal slave to mortal rage;
When I have seen the hungry ocean gain
Advantage on the kingdom of the shore,
And the firm soil win of the watery main,
Increasing store with loss, and loss with store;
When I have seen such interchange of state,
Or state itself confounded to decay;
Ruin hath taught me thus to ruminate
That Time will come and take my love away.
   This thought is as a death which cannot choose
   But weep to have that which it fears to lose.

what it means

The poet contemplates again how time buries all things and
pushes both men and nature into destruction. But
here, he has no optimism to offer. He simply
weeps at the thought of losing his love, a
thought that feels like death.

fact

Most of Shakespeare's plays
were set in Spain, the United
Kingdom, Italy and many ancient
cities in Greece and Turkey.

Sonnet 30

When to the sessions of sweet silent thought
I summon up remembrance of things past,
I sigh the lack of many a thing I sought,
And with old woes new wail my dear time's waste:
Then can I drown an eye, unused to flow,
For precious friends hid in death's dateless night,
And weep afresh love's long since cancelled woe,
And moan the expense of many a vanished sight:
Then can I grieve at grievances foregone,
And heavily from woe to woe tell o'er
The sad account of fore-bemoaned moan,
Which I new pay as if not paid before.
But if the while I think on thee, dear friend,
All losses are restor'd and sorrows end.

what it means

The poet here is grieving his failures, wasted time, and lost loves. Drowning in tears over the past, he feels depressed over sorrows for which he has already shed tears. But when he thinks about his dear friend, he gets back everything he's lost. The past has been replaced by the youth.

fact

Racism and anti-Semitism are both present in Shakespeare's plays. Othello, of African descent, is continuously insulted for his appearance and ancestry by both friend and foe. In the **Merchant of Venice**, the Jewish moneylender Shylock is portrayed as greedy and conniving.

Sonnet 60

Like as the waves make towards the pebbled shore,
So do our minutes hasten to their end;
Each changing place with that which goes before,
In sequent toil all forwards do contend.
Nativity, once in the main of light,
Crawls to maturity, wherewith being crown'd,
Crooked eclipses 'gainst his glory fight,
And Time that gave doth now his gift confound.
Time doth transfix the flourish set on youth
And delves the parallels in beauty's brow,
Feeds on the rarities of nature's truth,
And nothing stands but for his scythe to mow:
   And yet to times in hope, my verse shall stand
   Praising thy worth, despite his cruel hand.

what it means

The poet rails against Time once again, which creates obstacles for
everything it touches. It pierces beauty and devours nature,
while each moment replaces the one that came before
it. Despite this, his poetry will last into the
future.

fact

Shakespeare's Elizabethan
England was a time of prosperity,
stability, and great artistic
achievement. The Church had lost
some of its power, and secular
plays were again allowed.

Sonnet 65

Since brass, nor stone, nor earth, nor boundless sea,
But sad mortality o'ersways their power,
How with this rage shall beauty hold a plea,
Whose action is no stronger than a flower?
O! how shall summer's honey breath hold out,
Against the wrackful siege of battering days,
When rocks impregnable are not so stout,
Nor gates of steel so strong but Time decays?
O fearful meditation! where, alack,
Shall Time's best jewel from Time's chest lie hid?
Or what strong hand can hold his swift foot back?
Or who his spoil of beauty can forbid?
O! none, unless this miracle have might,
That in black ink my love may still shine bright.

what it means

Continuing the theme of Sonnet 64, the poet wonders how
beauty can resist death when brass and stone cannot.
How can beauty, fragile and sweet, hold its own?
The poet decides to hide the youth's beauty
from death in the lines of his poetry.

fact

Many people in Shakespeare's
time believed in witches,
including King James VI of
Scotland (who became king in
1603 and enjoyed many of the
Bard's plays). Before he was
king, he wrote a book about the
supernatural in 1597.

Sonnet 66

Tired with all these, for restful death I cry,
As to behold desert a beggar born,
And needy nothing trimm'd in jollity,
And purest faith unhappily forsworn,
And gilded honour shamefully misplaced,
And maiden virtue rudely strumpeted,
And right perfection wrongfully disgraced,
And strength by limping sway disabled
And art made tongue-tied by authority,
And folly, doctor-like, controlling skill,
And simple truth miscalled simplicity,
And captive good attending captain ill:
 Tired with all these, from these would I be gone,
 Save that, to die, I leave my love alone.

what it means

The poet is frustrated with the hypocrisies of life. While good
people are beggars, many "needy nothing" gets everything.
Honors are bestowed on the wrong men, lives are ruined
with slander, and art is censored by authority.
Better to die, he writes, except that he would
leave his love alone in the world.

fact

Queen Elizabeth I, one of
Shakespeare's patrons, had an
astronomer named Dr. John Dee.
The doctor believed he could
speak to angels and had figured
out their language.

Sonnet 71

No longer mourn for me when I am dead
Than you shall hear the surly sullen bell
Give warning to the world that I am fled
From this vile world with vilest worms to dwell:
Nay, if you read this line, remember not
The hand that writ it, for I love you so,
That I in your sweet thoughts would be forgot,
If thinking on me then should make you woe.
O! if, I say, you look upon this verse,
When I perhaps compounded am with clay,
Do not so much as my poor name rehearse;
But let your love even with my life decay;
Lest the wise world should look into your moan,
And mock you with me after I am gone.

what it means

The poet advises the youth to forget him after his death,
even to forget that he wrote the sonnets. He would
rather his love forget him than become sad from his
memory. The world may use the poet's possibly
tarnished memory to mock the youth.

fact

There are actually four witches
in **Macbeth**. The fourth, Hecate,
is a witch queen who appears in
a scene often left out in today's
performances.

Sonnet 72

O! lest the world should task you to recite
What merit lived in me, that you should love
After my death,--dear love, forget me quite,
For you in me can nothing worthy prove.
Unless you would devise some virtuous lie,
To do more for me than mine own desert,
And hang more praise upon deceased I
Than niggard truth would willingly impart:
O! lest your true love may seem false in this
That you for love speak well of me untrue,
My name be buried where my body is,
And live no more to shame nor me nor you.

    For I am shamed by that which I bring forth,
    And so should you, to love things nothing worth.

what it means

Continuing from the previous sonnet, the poet tells the youth that
he should forget about him entirely after his death. As a
thing without worth, the youth should avoid praising
him. People will only shame him for loving the
poet, and the youth will be forced to tell
kind lies about him.

fact

Many in Shakespeare's time
believed in astrology, the practice
of looking to the stars and planets
to tell the future. In *Romeo
and Juliet*, Romeo very literally
believes that "some consequence
yet hanging in the stars" is a sign
of his downfall.

Sonnet 73

That time of year thou mayst in me behold
When yellow leaves, or none, or few, do hang
Upon those boughs which shake against the cold,
Bare ruined choirs, where late the sweet birds sang.
In me thou see'st the twilight of such day
As after sunset fadeth in the west;
Which by and by black night doth take away,
Death's second self, that seals up all in rest.
In me thou see'st the glowing of such fire,
That on the ashes of his youth doth lie,
As the death-bed, whereon it must expire,
Consumed with that which it was nourish'd by.
This thou perceiv'st, which makes thy love more strong,
To love that well, which thou must leave ere long.

what it means

The poet believes that the youth sees the sun setting on life
when he looks at him. Despite his old age, the youth's
love becomes stronger, since he will lose the poet
soon enough.

fact

Astrologers were sometimes
paid to be present when a child
was born to work out the star
pattern at the time of birth.
Parents were eager to hear signs
of their child's future.

Sonnet 74

But be contented when that fell arrest
Without all bail shall carry me away,
My life hath in this line some interest,
Which for memorial still with thee shall stay.
When thou reviewest this, thou dost review
The very part was consecrate to thee:
The earth can have but earth, which is his due;
My spirit is thine, the better part of me:
So then thou hast but lost the dregs of life,
The prey of worms, my body being dead;
The coward conquest of a wretch's knife,
Too base of thee to be remembered.
   The worth of that is that which it contains,
   And that is this, and this with thee remains.

what it means

Don't mourn for me, the poet again tells the youth. His life will
continue in his art, and the youth will always have those
lines of verse to remember him. His spirit belongs to
the youth, and his spirit will remain in the poem.

fact

About 1,000 oak trees were cut
from English forests to build
the original Globe Theatre.

Sonnet 81

Or I shall live your epitaph to make,
Or you survive when I in earth am rotten,
From hence your memory death cannot take,
Although in me each part will be forgotten.
Your name from hence immortal life shall have,
Though I, once gone, to all the world must die:
The earth can yield me but a common grave,
When you entombed in men's eyes shall lie.
Your monument shall be my gentle verse,
Which eyes not yet created shall o'er-read;
And tongues to be your being shall rehearse,
When all the breathers of this world are dead;
You still shall live, such virtue hath my pen,
Where breath most breathes, even in the mouths of men.

what it means

Shakespeare tells the youth that death will be kinder to him,
as he and his beauty will live on in his poems. He will
merely have a simple grave, however his pen will
make it so that the youth will be forever talked
about, living on in the thoughts and
voices of men.

fact

In Shakespeare's time, the Globe
Theatre could hold about 3,000
people. Today, people like safety
regulations and leg room, so the
Theatre holds 1,500 people.

Sonnet 92

But do thy worst to steal thyself away,
For term of life thou art assured mine;
And life no longer than thy love will stay,
For it depends upon that love of thine.
Then need I not to fear the worst of wrongs,
When in the least of them my life hath end.
I see a better state to me belongs
Than that which on thy humour doth depend:
Thou canst not vex me with inconstant mind,
Since that my life on thy revolt doth lie.
O what a happy title do I find,
Happy to have thy love, happy to die!
    But what's so blessed-fair that fears no blot?
    Thou mayst be false, and yet I know it not.

what it means

The poet is describing being rejected by the youth, but tells him
that it won't hurt him. It hurts him more to be dependent
on his fickle affections. With his love, he will be
happy, and without it, he will simply die.

fact

The cause of the bubonic plague
that often closed theaters was
blamed on bad air, the stars, and
God being upset. Today, we know
it was the result of fleas, rats and
bad hygiene.

Sonnet 106

When in the chronicle of wasted time
I see descriptions of the fairest wights,
And beauty making beautiful old rhyme,
In praise of ladies dead and lovely knights,
Then, in the blazon of sweet beauty's best,
Of hand, of foot, of lip, of eye, of brow,
I see their antique pen would have expressed
Even such a beauty as you master now.
So all their praises are but prophecies
Of this our time, all you prefiguring;
And for they looked but with divining eyes,
They had not skill enough your worth to sing:
For we, which now behold these present days,
Have eyes to wonder, but lack tongues to praise.

what it means

When the poet reads old poetry describing ravishing beauty, he sees the old writers were merely describing the youth. Their poetry is a premonition of the youth. Without divine inspiration, they wouldn't have the foresight or skill to predict his beauty, and writers in the present lack the divine skill to praise him.

fact

Though people didn't bathe as often in Shakespeare's time, they changed their clothes as often as possible. Perfumes for covering up wretched smells were also popular.

Sonnet 107

Not mine own fears, nor the prophetic soul
Of the wide world dreaming on things to come,
Can yet the lease of my true love control,
Supposed as forfeit to a confined doom.
The mortal moon hath her eclipse endured,
And the sad augurs mock their own presage;
Incertainties now crown themselves assured,
And peace proclaims olives of endless age.
Now with the drops of this most balmy time,
My love looks fresh, and Death to me subscribes,
Since, spite of him, I'll live in this poor rhyme,
While he insults o'er dull and speechless tribes:
   And thou in this shalt find thy monument,
   When tyrants' crests and tombs of brass are spent.

what it means

Shakespeare here writes that he and his beloved are defying the
expectations of the world. With doubts eclipsed, they are
fatefully reunited. With this blessing, they will live on in
his art and surpass the small-minded people who
wished them ill.

fact

Most Elizabethans wrote with a
quill if they knew how to write.
Quills were made with the
feather of a large bird, usually
a goose, which was sharpened
to a point and dipped into ink.
This method made writing a
slow process.

Sonnet 115

Those lines that I before have writ do lie,
Even those that said I could not love you dearer:
Yet then my judgment knew no reason why
My most full flame should afterwards burn clearer.
But reckoning Time, whose million'd accidents
Creep in 'twixt vows, and change decrees of kings,
Tan sacred beauty, blunt the sharp'st intents,
Divert strong minds to the course of altering things;
Alas! why, fearing of Time's tyranny,
Might I not then say, 'Now I love you best,'
When I was certain o'er incertainty,
Crowning the present, doubting of the rest?
Love is a babe, then might I not say so,
To give full growth to that which still doth grow?

what it means

The poet tells the youth that he has lied about his love having
reached its peak. He has doubts, he says, because a
million things could happen to sever their love. By
fearing the passage of time, he neglected to tell
the youth that his love is only growing,
burning brighter each day.

fact

Even paper was expensive in
Elizabethan times. The amount
of pages needed to write a play
(around 30 sheets) cost the same
as three trips to the theatre.

Sonnet 118

Like as, to make our appetites more keen,
With eager compounds we our palate urge;
As, to prevent our maladies unseen,
We sicken to shun sickness when we purge;
Even so, being full of your ne'er-cloying sweetness,
To bitter sauces did I frame my feeding;
And, sick of welfare, found a kind of meetness
To be diseased, ere that there was true needing.
Thus policy in love, to anticipate
The ills that were not, grew to faults assured,
And brought to medicine a healthful state
Which, rank of goodness, would by ill be cured;
   But thence I learn and find the lesson true,
   Drugs poison him that so fell sick of you.

what it means

The poet tries to explain his unfaithfulness by saying that he was
trying to maintain his love for the youth by avoiding him.
By moving on to others, he was hoping to become sick
of them and return to him. Again unnecessarily
fearing Time's effects on their love, he
became used to cheating.

fact

Most people didn't drink water
in the 16th and 17th centuries,
since it was unclean and often
made people sick. Instead adults
and children alike drank beer
with a low alcohol content.

" *If this be error, and upon me proved,*
I never writ, nor no man ever loved. "

Sonnet 116

Let me not to the marriage of true minds
Admit impediments. Love is not love
Which alters when it alteration finds,
Or bends with the remover to remove:
O, no! it is an ever-fixed mark,
That looks on tempests and is never shaken;
It is the star to every wandering bark,
Whose worth's unknown, although his height be taken.
Love's not Time's fool, though rosy lips and cheeks
Within his bending sickle's compass come;
Love alters not with his brief hours and weeks,
But bears it out even to the edge of doom.
   If this be error and upon me proved,
   I never writ, nor no man ever loved.

what it means

This sonnet is typically held as a testament to what love is supposed to be, defeating time with its constancy. As a "marriage of true minds," love cannot be decayed by time or struggle.

Sonnet 120

That you were once unkind befriends me now,
And for that sorrow, which I then did feel,
Needs must I under my transgression bow,
Unless my nerves were brass or hammered steel.
For if you were by my unkindness shaken,
As I by yours, you've passed a hell of time;
And I, a tyrant, have no leisure taken
To weigh how once I suffered in your crime.
O! that our night of woe might have remembered
My deepest sense, how hard true sorrow hits,
And soon to you, as you to me, then tendered
The humble salve, which wounded bosoms fits!
But that your trespass now becomes a fee;
Mine ransoms yours, and yours must ransom me.

what it means

The youth is upset with the poet for having been unfaithful, but the
poet advises him to reflect on the past. Though, yes, he should
have remembered how the youth's infidelity hurt him
and not done the same, the youth acted first. And
though the youth deserved a quick apology,
he will have to remain satisfied with
knowing the debt is paid.

fact

Elizabethan boys in upper class
families wore dresses until they
were seven. After that, they
would begin wearing britches.

Sonnet 123

No, Time, thou shalt not boast that I do change:
Thy pyramids built up with newer might
To me are nothing novel, nothing strange;
They are but dressings of a former sight.
Our dates are brief, and therefore we admire
What thou dost foist upon us that is old;
And rather make them born to our desire
Than think that we before have heard them told.
Thy registers and thee I both defy,
Not wondering at the present nor the past,
For thy records and what we see doth lie,
Made more or less by thy continual haste.
   This I do vow and this shall ever be;
   I will be true despite thy scythe and thee.

what it means

Shakespeare speaks to time directly, telling it that his love is not of
mortal matter. Though it may convince us to honor or dwell
on the past and present, he knows it is an illusion. Life
is short and he will not let time destroy his love
while he lives.

fact

The word 'love' appears 150
times in *Romeo and Juliet*.

Sonnet 124

If my dear love were but the child of state,
It might for Fortune's bastard be unfathered,
As subject to Time's love or to Time's hate,
Weeds among weeds, or flowers with flowers gathered.
No, it was builded far from accident;
It suffers not in smiling pomp, nor falls
Under the blow of thralled discontent,
Whereto th' inviting time our fashion calls:
It fears not policy, that heretic,
Which works on leases of short-number'd hours,
But all alone stands hugely politic,
That it nor grows with heat, nor drowns with showers.
To this I witness call the fools of time,
Which die for goodness, who have lived for crime.

what it means

If love had been created simply by circumstances, the poet
writes, then it would fade like time and fashion. But no,
his love was created outside of earthly time and
place, and cannot be touched by schemers. It
will last in good and bad times.

fact

Theatre companies performing
Shakespeare's plays could make
rudimentary special effects.
Rolling a cannonball across the
floor or beating drums offstage
would make a thundering noise.

Sonnet 125

Were't aught to me I bore the canopy,
With my extern the outward honouring,
Or laid great bases for eternity,
Which proves more short than waste or ruining?
Have I not seen dwellers on form and favour
Lose all and more by paying too much rent
For compound sweet, forgoing simple savour,
Pitiful thrivers, in their gazing spent?
No; let me be obsequious in thy heart,
And take thou my oblation, poor but free,
Which is not mixed with seconds, knows no art,
But mutual render, only me for thee.
  Hence, thou suborned informer! a true soul
  When most impeached stands least in thy control.

what it means

The poet here asks if honoring power, money or appearances
will be worth his time. The answer is no, as he has seen
too many pitiful people use up their lives on things
easily decayed by time. He will dedicate himself
only to the youth, and the only exchange
will be for each other's love.

fact

To make lightning flashes,
players threw resin powder into
a candle flame, which lit with a
flash. To make a lightning bolt, a
wire was attached from the roof
to the floor of the stage. Then a
firecracker was tied to the wire
and lit.

"Her audit (though delayed) answered must be,
And her quietus is to render thee."

Sonnet 126

O thou, my lovely boy, who in thy power
Dost hold Time's fickle glass, his sickle, hour;
Who hast by waning grown, and therein showest
Thy lovers withering, as thy sweet self growest.
If Nature, sovereign mistress over wrack,
As thou goest onwards still will pluck thee back,
She keeps thee to this purpose, that her skill
May time disgrace and wretched minutes kill.
Yet fear her, O thou minion of her pleasure!
She may detain, but not still keep, her treasure:
Her audit (though delayed) answered must be,
And her quietus is to render thee.

(   )
(   )

what it means

The poet admires the youth's continued beauty, even though he is growing older. He believes nature must be defending him against time's effects. His loveliness has been chosen to be preserved for now, but nature must eventually pay her debts.

The Dark Lady

Sonnet 127

In the old age black was not counted fair,
Or if it were, it bore not beauty's name;
But now is black beauty's successive heir,
And beauty slandered with a bastard shame:
For since each hand hath put on Nature's power,
Fairing the foul with Art's false borrowed face,
Sweet beauty hath no name, no holy bower,
But is profaned, if not lives in disgrace.
Therefore my mistress' eyes are raven black,
Her eyes so suited, and they mourners seem
At such who, not born fair, no beauty lack,
Sland'ring creation with a false esteem:
Yet so they mourn becoming of their woe,
That every tongue says beauty should look so.

what it means

Sonnet 127 begins the "Dark Lady" sequence, where Shakespeare
reflects on the dark passion and sensuality inspired by his
mistress. Here, he posits that his mistress' dark hair and
eyes are a sign of mourning for real beauty, which
has been overshadowed by false faces
created with cosmetics.

fact

While many scholars have tried to
guess the identity of the Dark Lady,
she has never been identified. The
possibilities include prostitutes, married
women, and noble ladies, but no one has
been able to confirm her identity.

Sonnet 128

How oft when thou, my music, music play'st,
Upon that blessed wood whose motion sounds
With thy sweet fingers when thou gently sway'st
The wiry concord that mine ear confounds,
Do I envy those jacks that nimble leap,
To kiss the tender inward of thy hand,
Whilst my poor lips which should that harvest reap,
At the wood's boldness by thee blushing stand!
To be so tickled, they would change their state
And situation with those dancing chips,
O'er whom thy fingers walk with gentle gait,
Making dead wood more bless'd than living lips.
　　Since saucy jacks so happy are in this,
　　Give them thy fingers, me thy lips to kiss.

what it means

In this sonnet, Shakespeare pokes fun at the various euphemisms that traditional sonneteers used to describe their desire for intimacy with their love. Rather than "kiss the tender inward of thy hand" he says, he'd rather have her "Give them thy fingers, me thy lips to kiss."

fact

Shakespeare played with the traditional sonnet form by playing with its themes and structure. Rather than focus solely on idealized, innocent love, he explored its negative and dark sides as well.

66 All this the world well knows; yet none knows well
To shun the heaven that leads men to this hell. 99

fact

Scholars aren't sure what Shakespeare was up to between 1585 and 1592, but they believe he moved to London, often living apart from his wife and children (possibly for some "lust in action").

Sonnet 129

The expense of spirit in a waste of shame
Is lust in action: and till action, lust
Is perjured, murderous, bloody, full of blame,
Savage, extreme, rude, cruel, not to trust;
Enjoyed no sooner but despised straight;
Past reason hunted; and no sooner had,
Past reason hated, as a swallowed bait,
On purpose laid to make the taker mad.
Mad in pursuit and in possession so;
Had, having, and in quest to have extreme;
A bliss in proof, and proved, a very woe;
Before, a joy proposed; behind a dream.
　All this the world well knows; yet none knows well
　To shun the heaven that leads men to this hell.

what it means

This famous sonnet describes the various feelings that arise from lust: shame, savagery, desperation and woe among them. He concludes that lust—and its fruits—is the "heaven that leads men to this hell."

Sonnet 130

My mistress' eyes are nothing like the sun;
Coral is far more red, than her lips red:
If snow be white, why then her breasts are dun;
If hairs be wires, black wires grow on her head.
I have seen roses damasked, red and white,
But no such roses see I in her cheeks;
And in some perfumes is there more delight
Than in the breath that from my mistress reeks.
I love to hear her speak, yet well I know
That music hath a far more pleasing sound:
I grant I never saw a goddess go,
My mistress, when she walks, treads on the ground:
And yet by heaven, I think my love as rare,
As any she belied with false compare.

what it means

Shakespeare here is parodying the traditional sonnet writer's
inclination to compare his beloved to all things
beautiful. Once again rallying again false
beauty, he contends that his love is rare
even if she is hardly perfect in
appearance.

fact

According to paintings, the
Bard may have worn a gold
hoop earring, a trendy hallmark of
bohemian lifestyle at the time.

Sonnet 131

Thou art as tyrannous, so as thou art,
As those whose beauties proudly make them cruel;
For well thou know'st to my dear doting heart
Thou art the fairest and most precious jewel.
Yet, in good faith, some say that thee behold,
Thy face hath not the power to make love groan;
To say they err I dare not be so bold,
Although I swear it to myself alone.
And to be sure that is not false I swear,
A thousand groans, but thinking on thy face,
One on another's neck, do witness bear
Thy black is fairest in my judgment's place.
    In nothing art thou black save in thy deeds,
    And thence this slander, as I think, proceeds.

what it means

In these sonnets, Shakespeare is concerned with beauty and its
implications. Here, he describes his mistress' beauty as being
lesser than the traditional fair ladies, but the intensity of
his desire is no less. He also comments that her
deeds are not so pure.

fact

Scholars aren't exactly sure
what Shakespeare looked like.
The information we have on his
appearance comes from 17th century
paintings that may not have been painted
when he was alive.

Sonnet 132

Thine eyes I love, and they, as pitying me,
Knowing thy heart torments me with disdain,
Have put on black and loving mourners be,
Looking with pretty ruth upon my pain.
And truly not the morning sun of heaven
Better becomes the grey cheeks of the east,
Nor that full star that ushers in the even,
Doth half that glory to the sober west,
As those two mourning eyes become thy face:
O! let it then as well beseem thy heart
To mourn for me since mourning doth thee grace,
And suit thy pity like in every part.
Then will I swear beauty herself is black,
And all they foul that thy complexion lack.

what it means

A typical sonnet theme had the Muse regard the writer with pity
because he desires her. While her aloof beauty was typically
attributed to chastity and high morals, Shakespeare
inverts this by saying that his mistress'
blackness (both in complexion and
morals) is more desirable.

fact

We don't quite know the
spelling of Shakespeare's name.
Documents show that he used
abbreviations, including Willm
Shakp, Willm Shakspeare, and Willm
Shaskpere.

Sonnet 133

Beshrew that heart that makes my heart to groan
For that deep wound it gives my friend and me!
Is't not enough to torture me alone,
But slave to slavery my sweet'st friend must be?
Me from myself thy cruel eye hath taken,
And my next self thou harder hast engrossed:
Of him, myself, and thee I am forsaken;
A torment thrice three-fold thus to be crossed.
Prison my heart in thy steel bosom's ward,
But then my friend's heart let my poor heart bail;
Whoe'er keeps me, let my heart be his guard;
Thou canst not then use rigour in my jail:
   And yet thou wilt; for I, being pent in thee,
   Perforce am thine, and all that is in me.

what it means

In this sonnet, a new problem is introduced: his beloved Fair Youth
has fallen for the Dark Lady. He laments the mistress'
destructive power, her fickle whims, and the hurt
they inflict on one another.

fact

In his will, Shakespeare left his wife
his "second-best" bed. Many have
taken this as a sign of his disinterest
in her, but scholars say the best bed in
a home was for guests, meaning that the
second-best would have been their marriage
bed—a possible sign of affection.

Sonnet 134

So now I have confessed that he is thine,
And I my self am mortgaged to thy will,
Myself I'll forfeit, so that other mine
Thou wilt restore to be my comfort still:
But thou wilt not, nor he will not be free,
For thou art covetous, and he is kind;
He learned but surety-like to write for me,
Under that bond that him as fast doth bind.
The statute of thy beauty thou wilt take,
Thou usurer, that put'st forth all to use,
And sue a friend came debtor for my sake;
So him I lose through my unkind abuse.
Him have I lost; thou hast both him and me:
He pays the whole, and yet am I not free.

what it means

This sonnet continues the theme of entanglement from 133.
Shakespeare describes the relationship between the three
in legal terms, not the idealized ones from previous
sonnets. The effect is "love" described as a series
of transactions that leave Shakespeare
as the losing party.

fact

The materials to make special
effects in plays included sulfur and
saltpeter (made from feces), which
smelled terrible when lit. This gunpowder
mixture was used in **Macbeth** while the
witches were making a spell. The air was
likely terrible to breathe for the audience.

Sonnet 135

Whoever hath her wish, thou hast thy Will,
And Will to boot, and Will in over-plus;
More than enough am I that vexed thee still,
To thy sweet will making addition thus.
Wilt thou, whose will is large and spacious,
Not once vouchsafe to hide my will in thine?
Shall will in others seem right gracious,
And in my will no fair acceptance shine?
The sea, all water, yet receives rain still,
And in abundance addeth to his store;
So thou, being rich in Will, add to thy Will
One will of mine, to make thy large will more.
  Let no unkind, no fair beseechers kill;
  Think all but one, and me in that one Will.

what it means

This one sounds a bit like nonsense until you realize the word "will" is serving multiple meanings here, nearly all of them bawdy. Here, Shakespeare is playfully asking why his mistress will not accept his advances, when her desire for men are quite enormous.

fact

London in Shakespeare's time was big and growing. From 1550 to 1600, the city grew from about 50,000 residents to about 200,000. Today, about 8.3 million people live in London.

Sonnet 136

If thy soul check thee that I come so near,
Swear to thy blind soul that I was thy Will,
And will, thy soul knows, is admitted there;
Thus far for love, my love-suit, sweet, fulfil.
Will, will fulfil the treasure of thy love,
Ay, fill it full with wills, and my will one.
In things of great receipt with ease we prove
Among a number one is reckoned none:
Then in the number let me pass untold,
Though in thy store's account I one must be;
For nothing hold me, so it please thee hold
That nothing me, a something sweet to thee:
Make but my name thy love, and love that still,
And then thou lovest me for my name is 'Will.

what it means

Sonnet 136 continues the wordplay on "Will" and the pushy
attempts for William to get into the mistress' bed. He
continues to insult her, asking why he shouldn't be
among her lovers, when she has room for so
many. And if she has "will," why not
love a bit of "Will"?

fact

London streets in the 16th
century were crowded and
narrow, harboring crime and
disease. In 1607, English poet John
Donne said it was "London, plaguey
London, full of danger and vice."

Sonnet 137

Thou blind fool, Love, what dost thou to mine eyes,
That they behold, and see not what they see?
They know what beauty is, see where it lies,
Yet what the best is take the worst to be.
If eyes, corrupt by over-partial looks,
Be anchored in the bay where all men ride,
Why of eyes' falsehood hast thou forged hooks,
Whereto the judgment of my heart is tied?
Why should my heart think that a several plot,
Which my heart knows the wide world's common place?
Or mine eyes, seeing this, say this is not,
To put fair truth upon so foul a face?
    In things right true my heart and eyes have erred,
    And to this false plague are they now transferred.

what it means

Here, Shakespeare is continuing his unflattering reflection on his mistress.
He asks, "What do I see in this woman?" He calls her common
and refers to himself as "anchored in the bay where all
men ride." Regardless, his infatuation continues.

fact

Plague struck most summers in
Shakespeare's time, and in 1593
about 10,000 Londoners died from it.

" Therefore I lie with her, and she with me,
And in our faults by lies we flattered be. "

Sonnet 138

When my love swears that she is made of truth,
I do believe her though I know she lies,
That she might think me some untutored youth,
Unlearned in the world's false subtleties.
Thus vainly thinking that she thinks me young,
Although she knows my days are past the best,
Simply I credit her false-speaking tongue:
On both sides thus is simple truth suppressed:
But wherefore says she not she is unjust?
And wherefore say not I that I am old?
O! love's best habit is in seeming trust,
And age in love, loves not to have years told:
    Therefore I lie with her, and she with me,
    And in our faults by lies we flattered be.

what it means

Sonnet 138 explores the theme of desiring to believe a lie, especially when in love. Though she lies about being only his, and he lies by saying he believes her, they both submit to it out of weakness and self-flattery.

Sonnet 139

O! call not me to justify the wrong
That thy unkindness lays upon my heart;
Wound me not with thine eye, but with thy tongue:
Use power with power, and slay me not by art,
Tell me thou lov'st elsewhere; but in my sight,
Dear heart, forbear to glance thine eye aside:
What need'st thou wound with cunning, when thy might
Is more than my o'erpressed defence can bide?
Let me excuse thee: ah! my love well knows
Her pretty looks have been mine enemies;
And therefore from my face she turns my foes,
That they elsewhere might dart their injuries:
Yet do not so; but since I am near slain,
Kill me outright with looks, and rid my pain.

what it means

Typically, sonneteers excused the cruelties of their loves, as
Shakespeare rose to defend the Fair Youth. But here, he
refuses to excuse her blatant dalliances with other men.
Halfway through the sonnet, however, he blames
her behavior on her looks, which will
inevitably bring him pain.

fact

From 1603 to 1613,
Shakespeare's theatre company
played at the court of King James
about 15 times per year.

Sonnet 140

Be wise as thou art cruel; do not press
My tongue-tied patience with too much disdain;
Lest sorrow lend me words, and words express
The manner of my pity-wanting pain.
If I might teach thee wit, better it were,
Though not to love, yet, love to tell me so;
As testy sick men, when their deaths be near,
No news but health from their physicians know;
For, if I should despair, I should grow mad,
And in my madness might speak ill of thee;
Now this ill-wresting world is grown so bad,
Mad slanderers by mad ears believed be.
   That I may not be so, nor thou belied,
   Bear thine eyes straight, though thy proud heart go wide.

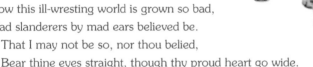

what it means

Shakespeare offers some cunning advice to his mistress: Even if you don't love me, pretend you do. The mistress, he writes, will avoid making him upset enough to speak ill of her. It's not the love proposed in Sonnet 116, by any means.

fact

People needing to cross the Thames River in the 16th century had another option besides the London Bridge: water taxis. About 3,000 water taxis operated in London at the time.

Sonnet 141

In faith I do not love thee with mine eyes,
For they in thee a thousand errors note;
But 'tis my heart that loves what they despise,
Who, in despite of view, is pleased to dote.
Nor are mine ears with thy tongue's tune delighted;
Nor tender feeling, to base touches prone,
Nor taste, nor smell, desire to be invited
To any sensual feast with thee alone:
But my five wits nor my five senses can
Dissuade one foolish heart from serving thee,
Who leaves unswayed the likeness of a man,
Thy proud heart's slave and vassal wretch to be:
Only my plague thus far I count my gain,
That she that makes me sin awards me pain.

what it means

The poet writes that his mistress is not a feast for the senses,
but that he is somehow still drawn to her, perhaps in
lust. At least she punishes him for his sins with
her lack of beauty and fidelity.

fact

Indoor theatres were a big
change that occurred in the
midst of Shakespeare's writing
career. The first permanent indoor
theatre, St. Paul's, was built in 1575.

Sonnet 142

Love is my sin, and thy dear virtue hate,
Hate of my sin, grounded on sinful loving:
O! but with mine compare thou thine own state,
And thou shalt find it merits not reproving;
Or, if it do, not from those lips of thine,
That have profaned their scarlet ornaments
And sealed false bonds of love as oft as mine,
Robbed others' beds' revenues of their rents.
Be it lawful I love thee, as thou lov'st those
Whom thine eyes woo as mine importune thee:
Root pity in thy heart, that, when it grows,
Thy pity may deserve to pitied be.
   If thou dost seek to have what thou dost hide,
   By self-example mayst thou be denied!

what it means

The mistress here has shown disdain for the poet's lust, and he counters
that she has committed the same sin many times over. He asks
that she have pity for his base desire, so that she'll
deserve her own pity.

fact

Indoor theatres were smaller
than outdoor ones, holding only
about 500 people, and were more
expensive to attend.

Sonnet 143

Lo, as a careful housewife runs to catch
One of her feathered creatures broke away,
Sets down her babe, and makes all swift dispatch
In pursuit of the thing she would have stay;
Whilst her neglected child holds her in chase,
Cries to catch her whose busy care is bent
To follow that which flies before her face,
Not prizing her poor infant's discontent;
So runn'st thou after that which flies from thee,
Whilst I thy babe chase thee afar behind;
But if thou catch thy hope, turn back to me,
And play the mother's part, kiss me, be kind;
So will I pray that thou mayst have thy 'Will,'
If thou turn back and my loud crying still.

what it means

The poet accuses the mistress of ignoring him, like a
housewife that is ignoring her child to catch a stray
hen. He tells her to turn back to him and be
kind, so that he'll stop crying for her.

fact

Because of the restrictions—
usually wealthier people
attended indoor theatres—it's
believed the audience was more
educated. Indoor plays had more
music, better props and more speeches
than action.

Sonnet 144

Two loves I have of comfort and despair,
Which like two spirits do suggest me still:
The better angel is a man right fair,
The worser spirit a woman coloured ill.
To win me soon to hell, my female evil,
Tempteth my better angel from my side,
And would corrupt my saint to be a devil,
Wooing his purity with her foul pride.
And whether that my angel be turned fiend,
Suspect I may, yet not directly tell;
But being both from me, both to each friend,
I guess one angel in another's hell:
    Yet this shall I ne'er know, but live in doubt,
    Till my bad angel fire my good one out.

what it means

The poet compares his two loves: the youth and the mistress. Both
lead him in different directions. The youth is a fair angel, while
the mistress is an ill-colored spirit. The mistress, in her
darkness, is trying to seduce the poet's angel. The
poet remains uncertain, though distraught,
by their infidelity.

fact

Like in an outdoor theatre, indoor
audiences could sit on cushions for
seats and buy snacks and beer. The
performances were lit by candles and
daylight from windows.

Sonnet 145

Those lips that Love's own hand did make,
Breathed forth the sound that said 'I hate',
To me that languished for her sake:
But when she saw my woeful state,
Straight in her heart did mercy come,
Chiding that tongue that ever sweet
Was used in giving gentle doom;
And taught it thus anew to greet;
'I hate' she altered with an end,
That followed it as gentle day,
Doth follow night, who like a fiend
From heaven to hell is flown away.
'I hate', from hate away she threw,
And saved my life, saying 'not you'.

what it means

Shakespeare has a tumultuous relationship with the mistress,
who turns from loving him to hating him in a single
breath. Here, she begins to say she hates him,
but finds some compassion, finishing her
sentence with "not you."

fact

Stools were allowed on the
stage, seats only purchased by
wealthy patrons who wanted to
see the play while being seen by the
audience. Royals, however, did not see
plays in public, and called the players to
their court instead.

Sonnet 147

My love is as a fever longing still,
For that which longer nurseth the disease;
Feeding on that which doth preserve the ill,
The uncertain sickly appetite to please.
My reason, the physician to my love,
Angry that his prescriptions are not kept,
Hath left me, and I desperate now approve
Desire is death, which physic did except.
Past cure I am, now Reason is past care,
And frantic-mad with evermore unrest;
My thoughts and my discourse as madmen's are,
At random from the truth vainly expressed;
  For I have sworn thee fair, and thought thee bright,
  Who art as black as hell, as dark as night.

what it means

Love is described here as a fever that prolongs disease, propping up
his immoral appetites. His desire for the mistress has turned
him mad, causing him to call her radiant when she is
actually "black as hell, and dark as night."

fact

Audiences were sometimes so
rowdy, that in 1612 magistrates
banned music at the end of plays at
the Fortune Theatre, because the crowd
had caused too many loud disturbances.

Sonnet 146

Poor soul, the centre of my sinful earth,
... ... these rebel powers that thee array
Why dost thou pine within and suffer dearth,
Painting thy outward walls so costly gay?
Why so large cost, having so short a lease,
Dost thou upon thy fading mansion spend?
Shall worms, inheritors of this excess,
Eat up thy charge? Is this thy body's end?
Then soul, live thou upon thy servant's loss,
And let that pine to aggravate thy store;
Buy terms divine in selling hours of dross;
Within be fed, without be rich no more:
So shall thou feed on Death, that feeds on men,
And Death once dead, there's no more dying then.

what it means

The poet laments that his soul sits in his sinful body, dressed on
the outside with fine clothing. He writes that his soul has
been starved for his body's pleasure, when it should
be the opposite. By feeding his soul instead, it
can defeat death, while his body will be
left to the worms.

fact

Audience interaction was more
common in Shakespeare's time
than in today's theatres. Audiences
booed and cheered with vigor at the
plays' twists and turns. Thieves and
pickpockets were commonly present, and
sometimes fights broke out.

Sonnet 148

O me! what eyes hath Love put in my head,
Which have no correspondence with true sight;
Or, if they have, where is my judgment fled,
That censures falsely what they see aright?
If that be fair whereon my false eyes dote,
What means the world to say it is not so?
If it be not, then love doth well denote
Love's eye is not so true as all men's: no,
How can it? O! how can Love's eye be true,
That is so vexed with watching and with tears?
No marvel then, though I mistake my view;
The sun itself sees not, till heaven clears.
   O cunning Love! with tears thou keep'st me blind,
   Lest eyes well-seeing thy foul faults should find.

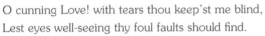

what it means

The theme of turning mad continues—the poet's eyes betray him. Though they tell him the mistress is desirable, the rest of the world does not. With her fickle treatment of him, he spends days in tears, and his eyes cannot see her faults.

fact

Plays typically had short runs and then were quickly replaced. For example, between 1560 and 1640 about 3,000 new plays were written.

Sonnet 149

Canst thou, O cruel! say I love thee not,
When I against myself with thee partake?
Do I not think on thee, when I forgot
Am of my self, all tyrant, for thy sake?
Who hateth thee that I do call my friend,
On whom frown'st thou that I do fawn upon,
Nay, if thou lour'st on me, do I not spend
Revenge upon myself with present moan?
What merit do I in my self respect,
That is so proud thy service to despise,
When all my best doth worship thy defect,
Commanded by the motion of thine eyes?
But, love, hate on, for now I know thy mind,
Those that can see thou lov'st, and I am blind.

what it means

Another frenzied sonnet has the poet wondering why his
mistress continues to reject him. Though he subjects
himself completely to her, he believes she loves
those who are less blind to her faults.

fact

Playwrights in the 16th century
typically borrowed plots from
classical writers or even each other.
Shakespeare's *The Taming of the
Shrew* was a re-write of a contemporary's
earlier play. That play was based on a plot
from the Roman writer Plautus.

Sonnet 150

O! from what power hast thou this powerful might,
With insufficiency my heart to sway?
To make me give the lie to my true sight,
And swear that brightness doth not grace the day?
Whence hast thou this becoming of things ill,
That in the very refuse of thy deeds
There is such strength and warrantise of skill,
That, in my mind, thy worst all best exceeds?
Who taught thee how to make me love thee more,
The more I hear and see just cause of hate?
O! though I love what others do abhor,
With others thou shouldst not abhor my state:
   If thy unworthiness raised love in me,
   More worthy I to be beloved of thee.

what it means

The poet continues wondering where the powerful hold of the
mistress originates. She makes darkness attractive and
convinces him to love her despite many reasons
to despise her. Yet, she has rejected him,
though he remains in her clutches.

fact

Censorship was institutionalized
at the time, and Shakespeare
occasionally criticizes it in his sonnets.
The Master of Revels, an official of the
royal court, had to grant a license for a play
to be performed. If it had political or religious
views he didn't like, it couldn't be performed.

Sonnet 151

Love is too young to know what conscience is,
Yet who knows not conscience is born of love?
Then, gentle cheater, urge not my amiss,
Lest guilty of my faults thy sweet self prove:
For, thou betraying me, I do betray
My nobler part to my gross body's treason;
My soul doth tell my body that he may
Triumph in love; flesh stays no farther reason,
But rising at thy name doth point out thee,
As his triumphant prize. Proud of this pride,
He is contented thy poor drudge to be,
To stand in thy affairs, fall by thy side.
No want of conscience hold it that I call
Her love, for whose dear love I rise and fall.

what it means

The poet here tries to determine the link between sexuality
and love, and concludes that they are intertwined—a
departure from traditional sonneteers like Petrarch.
Though his love with the mistress is tainted,
he believes it is of some worth, and
asks her not to reject him.

fact

To avoid offending the royal
censor, playwrights often set
their plays in imaginary countries
to avoid having their work banned,
while still making political or satirical
commentary.

Sonnet 153

Cupid laid by his brand and fell asleep:
A maid of Dian's this advantage found,
And his love-kindling fire did quickly steep
In a cold valley-fountain of that ground;
Which borrowed from this holy fire of Love,
A dateless lively heat, still to endure,
And grew a seething bath, which yet men prove
Against strange maladies a sovereign cure.
But at my mistress' eye Love's brand new-fired,
The boy for trial needs would touch my breast;
I, sick withal, the help of bath desired,
And thither hied, a sad distempered guest,

But found no cure, the bath for my help lies
Where Cupid got new fire; my mistress' eyes.

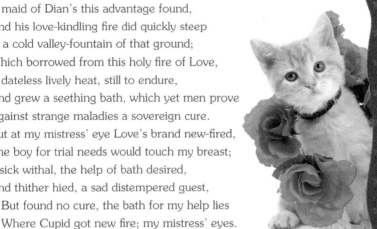

what it means

This more traditional sonnet is based on a Greek poem, and Shakespeare
adapts it to show that his love for the mistress, given by Cupid,
has become all-consuming. The only thing that can help,
he writes, is a glance from his mistress' eye.

fact

Shakespeare co-wrote
Henry VI Part 1 with an
unknown collaborator.

Sonnet 152

In loving thee thou know'st I am forsworn,
But thou art twice forsworn, to me love swearing;
In act thy bed-vow broke, and new faith torn,
In vowing new hate after new love bearing:
But why of two oaths' breach do I accuse thee,
When I break twenty? I am perjured most;
For all my vows are oaths but to misuse thee,
And all my honest faith in thee is lost:
For I have sworn deep oaths of thy deep kindness,
Oaths of thy love, thy truth, thy constancy;
And, to enlighten thee, gave eyes to blindness,
Or made them swear against the thing they see;
For I have sworn thee fair; more perjured eye,
To swear against the truth so foul a lie!

what it means

The sonnet serves as a farewell to the Dark Lady, but there is
little resolution to their tumultuous affair. Shakespeare
writes of the vows they have broken to those
they loved, of the lies he told himself to
make her seem worth it. But in the
end, he has simply lied twice
over: to her and himself.

fact

Playwrights were not usually
wealthy. They were paid a
one-time fee for selling a play to
an acting company. Since it was
common to co-write a work, they
had to share the money.

Sonnet 154

The little Love-god lying once asleep,
Laid by his side his heart-inflaming brand,
Whilst many nymphs that vowed chaste life to keep
Came tripping by; but in her maiden hand
The fairest votary took up that fire
Which many legions of true hearts had warmed;
And so the General of hot desire
Was, sleeping, by a virgin hand disarmed.
This brand she quenched in a cool well by,
Which from Love's fire took heat perpetual,
Growing a bath and healthful remedy,
For men diseased; but I, my mistress' thrall,
    Came there for cure and this by that I prove,
    Love's fire heats water, water cools not love.

what it means

The concluding sonnet, in the order placed by the publisher, continues
Shakespeare's adaptation of the Greek poem on Cupid. A maiden of the
goddess Diana, despite vowing to be chaste, was taken by desire and
broke her vow, possibly with a general. But, later, she was
able to quench this Cupid-given fire in water.
The poet's love for his mistress, he writes, is
immune to such a cure.

fact

Though writers weren't making
much money, it was still a living. A
playwright in the 1590s made about
five pounds for every play he sold—
the equivalent of a year's income for a
shopkeeper.

Beauty and Art

66 *So long as men can breathe, or eyes can see,
So long lives this, and this gives life to thee.* 99

Sonnet 18

Shall I compare thee to a summer's day?
Thou art more lovely and more temperate:
Rough winds do shake the darling buds of May,
And summer's lease hath all too short a date:
Sometime too hot the eye of heaven shines,
And often is his gold complexion dimmed,
And every fair from fair sometime declines,
By chance, or nature's changing course untrimmed:
But thy eternal summer shall not fade,
Nor lose possession of that fair thou ow'st,
Nor shall death brag thou wander'st in his shade,
When in eternal lines to time thou grow'st,
　　So long as men can breathe, or eyes can see,
　　So long lives this, and this gives life to thee.

what it means

This famous sonnet follows the procreation sequence, and here the poet places his bets on his art: the "summer's day" of the youth's beauty will never fade as a true summer does. It will continue forever in his poetry, and be more beautiful than it would in nature.

Sonnet 24

Mine eye hath played the painter and hath steeled,
Thy beauty's form in table of my heart;
My body is the frame wherein 'tis held,
And perspective that is best painter's art.
For through the painter must you see his skill,
To find where your true image pictured lies,
Which in my bosom's shop is hanging still,
That hath his windows glazed with thine eyes.
Now see what good turns eyes for eyes have done:
Mine eyes have drawn thy shape, and thine for me
Are windows to my breast, where-through the sun
Delights to peep, to gaze therein on thee;
Yet eyes this cunning want to grace their art,
They draw but what they see, know not the heart.

what it means

Shakespeare contemplates how he can draw a
picture of his love in his mind, but cannot see
into his heart. In his love's eyes, he can
see the reflection of his own love.
But he cannot know the youth's
mind and what he feels.

fact

Tragedies told sad stories that
often ended in death, like **Romeo
and Juliet**. The sad content in
Shakespeare's and other's plays was
balanced with blood and gore to
entertain the crowds.

Sonnet 28

How can I then return in happy plight,
That am debarred the benefit of rest?
When day's oppression is not eas'd by night,
But day by night and night by day oppressed,
And each, though enemies to either's reign,
Do in consent shake hands to torture me,
The one by toil, the other to complain
How far I toil, still farther off from thee.
I tell the day, to please him thou art bright,
And dost him grace when clouds do blot the heaven:
So flatter I the swart-complexion'd night,
When sparkling stars twire not thou gild'st the even.
　　But day doth daily draw my sorrows longer,
　　And night doth nightly make grief's length seem stronger.

what it means

The poet recounts many sleepless nights because
of the youth's absence. Though he tries to
think of him for comfort, the thought of
him being away weighs on his mind.

fact

Comedies had happy endings—
most often a wedding. Shakespeare
ended his Two Gentlemen of Verona
with two of them. Some comedies
were more satirical, like Ben Jonson's
The Alchemist.

Sonnet 32

If thou survive my well-contented day,
When that churl Death my bones with dust shall cover
And shalt by fortune once more re-survey
These poor rude lines of thy deceased lover,
Compare them with the bett'ring of the time,
And though they be outstripped by every pen,
Reserve them for my love, not for their rhyme,
Exceeded by the height of happier men.
O! then vouchsafe me but this loving thought:
'Had my friend's Muse grown with this growing age,
A dearer birth than this his love had brought,
To march in ranks of better equipage:
But since he died and poets better prove,
Theirs for their style I'll read, his for his love'.

what it means

If you live past my death, the poet writes, don't
think badly of my dated writing. Read my
work for its love of you, and consider
the advantages I didn't have. Read
newer writing for its style, but
mine for its sentiment.

fact

Actors' costumes very clearly
reflected social status. English
society was highly regimented, with
laws set in place to determine what
social classes could wear. For a less
important role, an actor sometimes
wore his own clothes.

Sonnet 37

As a decrepit father takes delight
To see his active child do deeds of youth,
So I, made lame by Fortune's dearest spite,
Take all my comfort of thy worth and truth;
For whether beauty, birth, or wealth, or wit,
Or any of these all, or all, or more,
Entitled in thy parts, do crowned sit,
I make my love engrafted to this store:
So then I am not lame, poor, nor despised,
Whilst that this shadow doth such substance give
That I in thy abundance am sufficed,
And by a part of all thy glory live.
  Look what is best, that best I wish in thee:
  This wish I have; then ten times happy me!

what it means

Like a child and decrepit parent, the poet draws
joy from seeing the youth's worth and good
character. Though he may be lame, old
and poor, he will live partly through
the young man's glory and beauty.

fact

Since all actors were men,
they wore women's clothing
onstage. They wore costumes
that reflected the social status of
the female character, including a
specific wig.

Sonnet 38

How can my muse want subject to invent,
While thou dost breathe, that pour'st into my verse
Thine own sweet argument, too excellent
For every vulgar paper to rehearse?
O! give thy self the thanks, if aught in me
Worthy perusal stand against thy sight;
For who's so dumb that cannot write to thee,
When thou thy self dost give invention light?
Be thou the tenth Muse, ten times more in worth
Than those old nine which rhymers invocate;
And he that calls on thee, let him bring forth
Eternal numbers to outlive long date.
If my slight muse do please these curious days,
The pain be mine, but thine shall be the praise.

what it means

Shakespeare here expresses some humility for his
writing, telling the youth that he should take
the credit for inspiring the words. You
should be the tenth muse, he writes.
The poet asks: Who couldn't
come up with something to write
with you as the inspiration?

fact

Acting companies ordered and reused
costumes as often as they could.
Scholars believe some actors left each
other costumes in their wills.

Sonnet 43

When most I wink, then do mine eyes best see,
For all the day they view things unrespected;
But when I sleep, in dreams they look on thee,
And darkly bright, are bright in dark directed.
Then thou, whose shadow shadows doth make bright,
How would thy shadow's form form happy show
To the clear day with thy much clearer light,
When to unseeing eyes thy shade shines so!
How would, I say, mine eyes be blessed made
By looking on thee in the living day,
When in dead night thy fair imperfect shade
Through heavy sleep on sightless eyes doth stay!
   All days are nights to see till I see thee,
   And nights bright days when dreams do show thee me.

what it means

My eyes see best when they're closed, the poet writes, since all day they look at things that are useless. When he dreams, the youth's beauty lights up the darkness. The daylight is dark without his beauty, and the night is bright when he dreams of him.

fact

A Swiss visitor to England in 1599 wrote that the upper classes sometimes left their clothing to their servants when they died. Servants were not allowed to wear clothes of a higher rank, so they sold them to acting companies.

Sonnet 46

Mine eye and heart are at a mortal war,
How to divide the conquest of thy sight;
Mine eye my heart thy picture's sight would bar,
My heart mine eye the freedom of that right.
My heart doth plead that thou in him dost lie,
A closet never pierced with crystal eyes,
But the defendant doth that plea deny,
And says in him thy fair appearance lies.
To 'cide this title is impannelled
A quest of thoughts, all tenants to the heart;
And by their verdict is determined
The clear eye's moiety, and the dear heart's part:
As thus: mine eye's due is thine outward part,
And my heart's right, thine inward love of heart.

what it means

The poet here discusses the conflict between his
eyes and heart in determining the youth's
beauty. The solution he comes to is this:
the eyes get to love his outward
appearance, while his heart will
love his inner beauty.

fact

Today, there are still productions of
Shakespeare's plays done at the Globe
with "original practices." That includes
men playing women's parts, as they
did when he was alive.

Sonnet 53

What is your substance, whereof are you made,
That millions of strange shadows on you tend?
Since every one hath, every one, one shade,
And you but one, can every shadow lend.
Describe Adonis, and the counterfeit
Is poorly imitated after you;
On Helen's cheek all art of beauty set,
And you in Grecian tires are painted new:
Speak of the spring, and foison of the year,
The one doth shadow of your beauty show,
The other as your bounty doth appear;
And you in every blessed shape we know.
    In all external grace you have some part,
    But you like none, none you, for constant heart.

what it means

Shakespeare writes that the youth's beauty can be
seen in every work of art and nature, from a
sculptor's Adonis to the spring season.
But all of these things are only an
imitation of the true source of all
grace, the youth.

fact

In Shakespeare's plays, make-up
and costumes worked together to
help the audience understand a
character easily. Make-up could also
transform the usually white actors
into dark-skinned Moors or other non-
English characters.

Sonnet 54

O! how much more doth beauty beauteous seem
By that sweet ornament which truth doth give.
The rose looks fair, but fairer we it deem
For that sweet odour, which doth in it live.
The canker blooms have full as deep a dye
As the perfumed tincture of the roses,
Hang on such thorns, and play as wantonly
When summer's breath their masked buds discloses:
But, for their virtue only is their show,
They live unwoo'd, and unrespected fade;
Die to themselves. Sweet roses do not so;
Of their sweet deaths are sweetest odours made:
And so of you, beauteous and lovely youth,
When that shall vade, my verse distills your truth.

what it means

The poet assures the youth that he will live on in his verse. Some flowers merely have their looks, so they die forgotten. But as the rose dies, the sweetest perfume is made. In the same way, the youth will inspire the Bard's poetry.

fact

Natural ingredients were used in actors' make-up, though they might seem a bit gross to modern players. Powdered hog bones and poppy oil were used to make boys' faces pale and more feminine.

Sonnet 55

Not marble, nor the gilded monuments
Of princes, shall outlive this powerful rhyme;
But you shall shine more bright in these contents
Than unswept stone, besmear'd with sluttish time.
When wasteful war shall statues overturn,
And broils root out the work of masonry,
Nor Mars his sword, nor war's quick fire shall burn
The living record of your memory.
'Gainst death, and all oblivious enmity
Shall you pace forth; your praise shall still find room
Even in the eyes of all posterity
That wear this world out to the ending doom.
  So, till the judgment that yourself arise,
  You live in this, and dwell in lovers' eyes.

what it means

While time will destroy statues and stone, the
poet's rhymes will outlive all the material.
The eyes of future lovers will praise the
youth and, of course, the poet.

fact

According to Shakespeare scholar
Louis Marder, the Bard used over
7,000 distinct words (more than the
entire Bible) only once in his writing.

Sonnet 59

If there be nothing new, but that which is
Hath been before, how are our brains beguil'd,
Which labouring for invention bear amiss
The second burthen of a former child.
Oh that record could with a backward look,
Even of five hundred courses of the sun,
Show me your image in some antique book,
Since mind at first in character was done,
That I might see what the old world could say
To this composed wonder of your frame;
Whether we are mended, or where better they,
Or whether revolution be the same.
Oh sure I am the wits of former days,
To subjects worse have given admiring praise.

what it means

If every good idea has already been written,
Shakespeare writes, then all new art will
merely be an imitation. But there's no
way to know, because the youth
didn't exist in the past. The writers
of the past likely did not have a
worthy subject like the youth.

fact

Over half a million tickets a year
are sold for the Royal Shakespeare
Company's productions at their
theatres in London, Newcastle and
Stratford-upon-Avon.

Sonnet 67

Ah! wherefore with infection should he live,
And with his presence grace impiety,
That sin by him advantage should achieve,
And lace itself with his society?
Why should false painting imitate his cheek,
And steal dead seeming of his living hue?
Why should poor beauty indirectly seek
Roses of shadow, since his rose is true?
Why should he live, now Nature bankrupt is,
Beggared of blood to blush through lively veins?
For she hath no exchequer now but his,
And proud of many, lives upon his gains.
  O! him she stores, to show what wealth she had
  In days long since, before these last so bad.

what it means

The poet laments that his love should have to live
among so many sinners and corrupt people.
Why should bad painters get to poorly
imitate his cheek? Why should fakery
like make-up allow people to imitate
his beauty? It must be, he says,
because Nature has run out of
beauty for everyone else, and
needs to borrow the youth's.

fact

While some claim Shakespeare
was left-handed, studies of his
handwriting show he wrote
comfortably with his right and was
naturally right-handed. A bust put up
in the church of his burial site has him
holding a quill in his right hand.

66 And him as for a map doth nature store,
To show false art what beauty was of yore. 99

Sonnet 68

Thus is his cheek the map of days outworn,
When beauty lived and died as flow'rs do now,
Before these bastard signs of fair were born,
Or durst inhabit on a living brow;
Before the golden tresses of the dead,
The right of sepulchers, were shorn away,
To live a second life on second head;
Ere beauty's dead fleece made another gay.
In him those holy ántique hours are seen,
Without all ornament, itself and true,
Making no summer of another's green,
Robbing no old to dress his beauty new;
   And him as for a map doth nature store,
   To show false art what beauty was of yore.

what it means

Shakespeare praises the youth's old fashioned beauty here—in his time people take golden hair from corpses to make themselves beautiful. In the youth's face is real beauty without ornament, cosmetics or wigs.

Sonnet 69

Those parts of thee that the world's eye doth view
Want nothing that the thought of hearts can mend;
All tongues, the voice of souls, give thee that due,
Uttering bare truth, even so as foes commend.
Thy outward thus with outward praise is crown'd;
But those same tongues, that give thee so thine own,
In other accents do this praise confound
By seeing farther than the eye hath shown.
They look into the beauty of thy mind,
And that in guess they measure by thy deeds;
Then, churls, their thoughts, although their eyes were kind,
To thy fair flower add the rank smell of weeds:
But why thy odour matcheth not thy show,
The soil is this, that thou dost common grow.

what it means

People are likely to praise your beautiful
appearance, the poet advises the youth. But
if they are of poor character, they will
misjudge your inner good with their
ill thoughts. And if that's the case,
they are common weeds.

fact

No known artifacts of Shakespeare's
personal items or any from his
family survive today. Many people
made wild claims in the 18th and
19th centuries regarding chairs that
may have belonged to him, but
none have been substantiated.

Sonnet 70

That thou art blamed shall not be thy defect,
For slander's mark was ever yet the fair;
The ornament of beauty is suspect,
A crow that flies in heaven's sweetest air.
So thou be good, slander doth but approve
Thy worth the greater, being wooed of time;
For canker vice the sweetest buds doth love,
And thou present'st a pure unstained prime.
Thou hast passed by the ambush of young days
Either not assailed, or victor being charged;
Yet this thy praise cannot be so thy praise,
To tie up envy, evermore enlarged,

    If some suspect of ill masked not thy show,
    Then thou alone kingdoms of hearts shouldst owe.

what it means

The poet continues the theme of ignoring public
opinion. Beauty and good will always be
attacked by those who are of less worth.
If people were less inclined to think
ill of you, the world would owe
you its heart.

fact

There has been much speculation
about Shakespeare's "lost years."
Writings from the time show he
may have been a schoolteacher for
a few years.

Sonnet 76

Why is my verse so barren of new pride,
So far from variation or quick change?
Why with the time do I not glance aside
To new-found methods, and to compounds strange?
Why write I still all one, ever the same,
And keep invention in a noted weed,
That every word doth almost tell my name,
Showing their birth, and where they did proceed?
O! know sweet love I always write of you,
And you and love are still my argument;
So all my best is dressing old words new,
Spending again what is already spent:
For as the sun is daily new and old,
So is my love still telling what is told.

what it means

The poet tells the youth why he is straightforward
in his writing, he wants only to write of his
beauty. While other writers try strange
combinations and flatter their egos,
he will only find new ways to
write about his love. The sun
each day becomes new and
old, and so will his poetry.

fact

While Italy is a prominent setting in
Shakespeare's plays, it's unknown
if he ever traveled there. Italian
literature was widely read at the time,
and it's possible he got his Italian
references from an Italian tutor to
Shakespeare's patron.

Sonnet 78

So oft have I invoked thee for my Muse,
And found such fair assistance in my verse
As every alien pen hath got my use
And under thee their poesy disperse.
Thine eyes, that taught the dumb on high to sing
And heavy ignorance aloft to fly,
Have added feathers to the learned's wing
And given grace a double majesty.
Yet be most proud of that which I compile,
Whose influence is thine, and born of thee:
In others' works thou dost but mend the style,
And arts with thy sweet graces graced be;
    But thou art all my art, and dost advance
    As high as learning, my rude ignorance.

what it means

Shakespeare mentions the "Rival Poets" here, who have taken up his habit of writing about the youth. He proposes that the youth should be proud, since he has inspired these ignorant, dumb writers to write something of worth---especially Shakespeare.

fact

It is believed that Queen Elizabeth I really liked the character of Falstaff in *Henry IV, Part 1*, and asked Shakespeare to write a play of him in love. This may have inspired *The Merry Wives of Windsor*.

Sonnet 79

Whilst I alone did call upon thy aid,
My verse alone had all thy gentle grace;
But now my gracious numbers are decayed,
And my sick Muse doth give an other place.
I grant, sweet love, thy lovely argument
Deserves the travail of a worthier pen;
Yet what of thee thy poet doth invent
He robs thee of, and pays it thee again.
He lends thee virtue, and he stole that word
From thy behaviour; beauty doth he give,
And found it in thy cheek: he can afford
No praise to thee, but what in thee doth live.
Then thank him not for that which he doth say,
Since what he owes thee, thou thyself dost pay.

what it means

The poet says that his poems no longer meet
the expectations of the youth. But whatever
new writer he finds, he will only be
regurgitating the youth's beauty in
words. If he calls him virtuous,
he only learned the word from
watching the youth.

fact

The average height of a 16th
century person was about two
inches shorter than people of today.
Unfortunately, we have little idea of
what Shakespeare looked like or how
tall he was.

Sonnet 83

I never saw that you did painting need,
And therefore to your fair no painting set;
I found, or thought I found, you did exceed
The barren tender of a poet's debt:
And therefore have I slept in your report,
That you yourself, being extant, well might show
How far a modern quill doth come too short,
Speaking of worth, what worth in you doth grow.
This silence for my sin you did impute,
Which shall be most my glory being dumb;
For I impair not beauty being mute,
When others would give life, and bring a tomb.
    There lives more life in one of your fair eyes
    Than both your poets can in praise devise.

what it means

Shakespeare tries to excuse his supposedly plain
writing by saying that he didn't believe
the youth's beauty needed elaborate
praise—it spoke for itself. Though
he may not be commended for his
silence, at least he didn't tarnish
the youth's qualities with false
praise.

fact

A 1926 sketchbook belonging
to Hitler included a stage design
for *Julius Caesar*. Apparently, the
Führer was a fan of the Bard, but
it's unlikely the feeling would have
been mutual.

" Then if he thrive and I be cast away,
The worst was this, my love was my decay. "

Sonnet 80

O! how I faint when I of you do write,
Knowing a better spirit doth use your name,
And in the praise thereof spends all his might,
To make me tongue-tied speaking of your fame.
But since your worth, wide as the ocean is,
The humble as the proudest sail doth bear,
My saucy bark, inferior far to his,
On your broad main doth wilfully appear.
Your shallowest help will hold me up afloat,
Whilst he upon your soundless deep doth ride;
Or, being wracked, I am a worthless boat,
He of tall building, and of goodly pride:
　　Then if he thrive and I be cast away,
　　The worst was this, my love was my decay.

what it means

The "Rival Poet" sonnets continue with the poet's lament that he has to compete for the youth's attention. While the rival is a well-built boat, he is an inferior little one. But if he is shipwrecked in his tiny vessel, at least it was for the youth's love.

Sonnet 84

Who is it that says most, which can say more,
Than this rich praise, that you alone, are you,
In whose confine immured is the store
Which should example where your equal grew?
Lean penury within that pen doth dwell
That to his subject lends not some small glory;
But he that writes of you, if he can tell
That you are you, so dignifies his story.
Let him but copy what in you is writ,
Not making worse what nature made so clear,
And such a counterpart shall fame his wit,
Making his style admired every where.
You to your beauteous blessings add a curse,
Being fond on praise, which makes your praises worse.

what it means

If all beauty is stored in the youth, the poet
writes, what can a writer add to that infinite
store? Whoever writes about the youth
will only be adding worth to their
writing, and add nothing to his
beauty. The youth will gain little
from being "fond on praise."

fact

Many famous opera composers,
including Verdi and Mozart, tried to
adapt Shakespeare's plays into operas.
Verdi attempted *King Lear*, while
Mozart tried to create a version of *The
Tempest*. Neither succeeded, probably
finding the task too daunting.

Sonnet 85

My tongue-tied Muse in manners holds her still,
While comments of your praise richly compiled,
Reserve thy character with golden quill,
And precious phrase by all the Muses filed.
I think good thoughts, whilst others write good words,
And like unlettered clerk still cry 'Amen'
To every hymn that able spirit affords,
In polished form of well-refined pen.
Hearing you praised, I say ''tis so, 'tis true,'
And to the most of praise add something more;
But that is in my thought, whose love to you,
Though words come hindmost, holds his rank before.
  Then others, for the breath of words respect,
  Me for my dumb thoughts, speaking in effect.

what it means

The poet explains his silence further: he loves the
youth the most even if he speaks least. While
others express their fondness in writing
and praise, he does it in his actions.

fact

The first fan-made performance of
one of Shakespeare's plays took place
in Kent in 1623. The English politician
Sir Edward Dering paid a rector
to write out **Henry IV** for a private
performance in his home. He even
bought wigs and beards for his cast.

Sonnet 86

Was it the proud full sail of his great verse,
Bound for the prize of all too precious you,
That did my ripe thoughts in my brain inhearse,
Making their tomb the womb wherein they grew?
Was it his spirit, by spirits taught to write
Above a mortal pitch, that struck me dead?
No, neither he, nor his compeers by night
Giving him aid, my verse astonished.
He, nor that affable familiar ghost
Which nightly gulls him with intelligence,
As victors of my silence cannot boast;
I was not sick of any fear from thence:
But when your countenance filled up his line,
Then lacked I matter; that enfeebled mine.

what it means

Shakespeare asks: Was it the great verse my rival
wrote that killed my inspiration? No, he is
not afraid of the "Rival Poet." It was the
youth's praise of the rival's writing
that silenced and hurt him.

fact

Shakespeare was the first to name a
fictional character "Jessica," who was
Shylock's daughter in **The Merchant
of Venice**.

Sonnet 96

Some say thy fault is youth, some wantonness;
Some say thy grace is youth and gentle sport;
Both grace and faults are lov'd of more and less:
Thou mak'st faults graces that to thee resort.
As on the finger of a throned queen
The basest jewel will be well esteem'd,
So are those errors that in thee are seen
To truths translated, and for true things deem'd.
How many lambs might the stern wolf betray,
If like a lamb he could his looks translate!
How many gazers mightst thou lead away,
If thou wouldst use the strength of all thy state!
　But do not so, I love thee in such sort,
　As thou being mine, mine is thy good report.

what it means

Shakespeare explores the youth's qualities:
wantonness and lust. Some say it is a
problem, while others find it charming.
Like a worthless jewel on the neck of
a queen, the youth's sins become
jewels to others. Because of this,
he writes, the youth must not
trick others with his beauty

fact

The Bard has had countless
influence over writers the world
over. William Faulkner, Aldous
Huxley, Vladimir Nabokov, and
David Foster Wallace all titled
one of their works from a line in
Shakespeare.

Sonnet 94

They that have power to hurt, and will do none,
That do not do the thing they most do show,
Who, moving others, are themselves as stone,
Unmoved, cold, and to temptation slow;
They rightly do inherit heaven's graces,
And husband nature's riches from expense;
They are the lords and owners of their faces,
Others, but stewards of their excellence.
The summer's flower is to the summer sweet,
Though to itself, it only live and die,
But if that flower with base infection meet,
The basest weed outbraves his dignity:
For sweetest things turn sourest by their deeds;
Lilies that fester, smell far worse than weeds.

what it means

The poet here discusses the responsibilities of beauty: those who have self-control and don't abuse their seductive powers will "inherit heaven's graces." The sweetest flowers, he writes, will become worse than weeds if they are immoral.

fact

English playwright David Garrick edited **Romeo and Juliet** to remove the character of Rosaline, Romeo's love before he suddenly falls for Juliet. His 18th century version was popular for over a hundred years since it glossed over the fact that Romeo was a bit of a dumb, rash teenager.

Sonnet 97

How like a winter hath my absence been
From thee, the pleasure of the fleeting year!
What freezings have I felt, what dark days seen!
What old December's bareness everywhere!
And yet this time removed was summer's time;
The teeming autumn, big with rich increase,
Bearing the wanton burden of the prime,
Like widow'd wombs after their lords' decease:
Yet this abundant issue seemed to me
But hope of orphans, and unfathered fruit;
For summer and his pleasures wait on thee,
And, thou away, the very birds are mute:
   Or, if they sing, 'tis with so dull a cheer,
   That leaves look pale, dreading the winter's near.

what it means

The poet describes a period apart from the youth
as a harsh winter, though warm seasons have
passed. Summer and all its pleasures
depend on the youth's presence.
Even birds fail to sing when his
warmth is gone.

fact

Not every writer has been dutifully
fond of Shakespeare. Leo Tolstoy
wrote a whole book about him,
railing against his apparently tedious
writing style. In an essay, George
Orwell addressed Tolstoy's claims,
saying that the worth of Shakespeare's
writing lies in its poetry, rather than its
drama.

Sonnet 99

The forward violet thus did I chide:
Sweet thief, whence didst thou steal thy sweet that smells,
If not from my love's breath? The purple pride
Which on thy soft cheek for complexion dwells
In my love's veins thou hast too grossly dy'd.
The lily I condemned for thy hand,
And buds of marjoram had stol'n thy hair;
The roses fearfully on thorns did stand,
One blushing shame, another white despair;
A third, nor red nor white, had stol'n of both,
And to his robbery had annexed thy breath;
But, for his theft, in pride of all his growth
A vengeful canker eat him up to death.
More flowers I noted, yet I none could see,
But sweet, or colour it had stol'n from thee.

what it means

In the youth's absence, the poet condemns
flowers for stealing the youth's beauty. Like
a colorless unattractive rose, they steal
the youth's color, his curly hair and
even his smell. Though the poet
observes their beauty, it pales in
comparison to him.

fact

Not only have the Globe Theatre's
players experimented with original
practices in the way they stage
Shakespeare's plays, they've tried original
pronunciation. This requires actors to
pronounce words in a 400-year-old
English accent. For example, the word
"proved" in Sonnet 116 is intended to
rhyme with "loved."

Sonnet 100

Where art thou Muse that thou forget'st so long,
To speak of that which gives thee all thy might?
Spend'st thou thy fury on some worthless song,
Darkening thy power to lend base subjects light?
Return forgetful Muse, and straight redeem,
In gentle numbers time so idly spent;
Sing to the ear that doth thy lays esteem
And gives thy pen both skill and argument.
Rise, resty Muse, my love's sweet face survey,
If Time have any wrinkle graven there;
If any, be a satire to decay,
And make Time's spoils despised every where.
　　Give my love fame faster than Time wastes life,
　　So thou prevent'st his scythe and crooked knife.

what it means

Like many sonneteers, Shakespeare implores the muses to give him inspiration. He needs to write, he says, to prevent time's destructive power on the youth's beauty. Do not waste time on worthless poems, he tells the muse, but provide the words he needs to immortalize his love.

fact

In all of the Beatles' songs, there is only one reference to Shakespeare—the fadeout from "I Am the Walrus" features a line from a *King Lear* radio broadcast.

Sonnet 101

O truant Muse what shall be thy amends
For thy neglect of truth in beauty dyed?
Both truth and beauty on my love depends;
So dost thou too, and therein dignified.
Make answer Muse: wilt thou not haply say,
'Truth needs no colour, with his colour fixed;
Beauty no pencil, beauty's truth to lay;
But best is best, if never intermixed'?
Because he needs no praise, wilt thou be dumb?
Excuse not silence so, for't lies in thee
To make him much outlive a gilded tomb
And to be praised of ages yet to be.
Then do thy office, Muse; I teach thee how
To make him seem, long hence, as he shows now.

what it means

Continuing from Sonnet 100, he tells the muse
to make amends for her neglect. Truth and
beauty depend on the beloved, and must
be preserved for the future.

fact

A piece of Shakespeare folklore
claims that the newly-married
Shakespeare stole a deer from a
wealthy Stratford resident, then was
whipped by him and fled in shame to
London. The rumor appears to have
started in the 17th century and was
accepted as fact for centuries later,
though today scholars say there's no
evidence to support it.

Sonnet 103

Alack! what poverty my Muse brings forth,
That having such a scope to show her pride,
The argument all bare is of more worth
Than when it hath my added praise beside!
O! blame me not, if I no more can write!
Look in your glass, and there appears a face
That over-goes my blunt invention quite,
Dulling my lines, and doing me disgrace.
Were it not sinful then, striving to mend,
To mar the subject that before was well?
For to no other pass my verses tend
Than of your graces and your gifts to tell;
    And more, much more, than in my verse can sit,
    Your own glass shows you when you look in it.

what it means

Shakespeare calls himself a bad poet, since he
cannot write anything that illuminates further
on the youth's graces. Why write if it
won't capture the subject properly?
He tells the youth to look in the
mirror, because there will be
more beauty there than in his
poetry.

fact

The United Nations declared April
23rd World Book Day in honor
of many authors who passed away
on that date, including Miguel de
Cervantes and, of course, William
Shakespeare. They actually died 11
days apart using a modern calendar.

Sonnet 105

Let not my love be called idolatry,
Nor my beloved as an idol show,
Since all alike my songs and praises be
To one, of one, still such, and ever so.
Kind is my love to-day, to-morrow kind,
Still constant in a wondrous excellence;
Therefore my verse to constancy confined,
One thing expressing, leaves out difference.
Fair, kind, and true, is all my argument,
Fair, kind, and true, varying to other words;
And in this change is my invention spent,
Three themes in one, which wondrous scope affords.
Fair, kind, and true, have often lived alone,
Which three till now, never kept seat in one.

what it means

The poet writes that no one can call his poetry
idolatry, because all his praises are directed at
the same subject: the youth. His writing
will only consist of fair, kind and true
things because of their subject.
Though they have been thought
to be separate qualities, they all
exist perfectly in the youth.

fact

Stratford-upon-Avon had many
former Catholics in Shakespeare's
time, and government spies were
active in the area to sniff them out for
signs of treason. Their reports show
that many Catholic priests were still
active in the area, and possibly married
Shakespeare and his wife.

Sonnet 113

Since I left you, mine eye is in my mind;
And that which governs me to go about
Doth part his function and is partly blind,
Seems seeing, but effectually is out;
For it no form delivers to the heart
Of bird, of flower, or shape which it doth latch:
Of his quick objects hath the mind no part,
Nor his own vision holds what it doth catch;
For if it see the rud'st or gentlest sight,
The most sweet favour or deformed'st creature,
The mountain or the sea, the day or night,
The crow, or dove, it shapes them to your feature.
　　Incapable of more, replete with you,
　　My most true mind thus maketh mine eye untrue.

what it means

Shakespeare has left the youth for some time, and
is absorbed in thoughts of him. Even when
he sees something ugly or beautiful,
his mind's eye transforms it into the
youth. Filled with thoughts of him,
everything else becomes skewed.

fact

Shakespeare wasn't much of a
churchgoer, maybe out of personal
preference or Catholic rebellion.
Many areas of London required
church attendance, but no records
survive showing he attended church
near his known residences in the city.

Sonnet 114

Or whether doth my mind, being crowned with you,
Drink up the monarch's plague, this flattery?
Or whether shall I say, mine eye saith true,
And that your love taught it this alchemy,
To make of monsters and things indigest
Such cherubins as your sweet self resemble,
Creating every bad a perfect best,
As fast as objects to his beams assemble?
O! 'tis the first, 'tis flattery in my seeing,
And my great mind most kingly drinks it up:
Mine eye well knows what with his gust is 'greeing,
And to his palate doth prepare the cup:
If it be poisoned, 'tis the lesser sin
That mine eye loves it and doth first begin.

what it means

The poet wonders if he has become consumed
with delusions because of the youth's
flattering love. Or is it that the youth's
love is alchemy that allows him to
transform everything into his love's
image? Though these visions are
false, his eyes can be excused
for their eager love.

fact

Later in his life, Shakespeare appeared
more frequently in London's public
records, and was even called for a
deposition in a court case. He had
served as a mediator in a dowry dispute
for a family with whom he lived, and
his questioning was logged by the
court—a rare record of his speech.

Sonnet 119

What potions have I drunk of Siren tears,
Distilled from limbecks foul as hell within,
Applying fears to hopes, and hopes to fears,
Still losing when I saw myself to win!
What wretched errors hath my heart committed,
Whilst it hath thought itself so blessed never!
How have mine eyes out of their spheres been fitted,
In the distraction of this madding fever!
O benefit of ill! now I find true
That better is by evil still made better;
And ruined love, when it is built anew,
Grows fairer than at first, more strong, far greater.
   So I return rebuked to my content,
   And gain by ill thrice more than I have spent.

what it means

A period of infatuation has set upon Shakespeare,
which has become like a maddening
fever. Having committed an unknown
infidelity, he realizes that love
that is ruined can be rebuilt into
something more beautiful. He
will return to his love and reap
the benefits of his wrong.

fact

The only surviving letter to
Shakespeare comes from his friend
Richard Quiney, dating back to
1597. It's possible that William was
a moneylender on the side, like his
father, since Quiney was asking him
to borrow money.

66 *Unless this general evil they maintain,*
All men are bad and in their badness reign. 99

Sonnet 121

'Tis better to be vile than vile esteemed,
When not to be receives reproach of being;
And the just pleasure lost, which is so deemed
Not by our feeling, but by others' seeing:
For why should others' false adulterate eyes
Give salutation to my sportive blood?
Or on my frailties why are frailer spies,
Which in their wills count bad what I think good?
No, I am that I am, and they that level
At my abuses reckon up their own:
I may be straight though they themselves be bevel;
By their rank thoughts, my deeds must not be shown;
Unless this general evil they maintain,
All men are bad and in their badness reign.

what it means

It's better to do wrong, writes the poet, than to merely have people accuse you of it. If the sin they say you committed never occurred, you didn't even get to have fun being bad. Why should others get to judge, when they are immoral too? They simply reveal their inner ugliness with accusations.

About the Author

William Shakespeare, widely considered one of the greatest dramatists in the English language, was born around April 23, 1564 in Stratford-upon-Avon. His works include 38 plays, 154 sonnets, two narrative poems, and other works that have been lost to history.

His friend, Ben Jonson, wrote that the Bard "was not of an age, but for all time." With his works translated and performed in over 80 languages around the world, Jonson's words ring true. Four hundred years later, we're still asking, "Shall I compare thee to a summer's day?"

Sources

"Shakespeare's Life." Folger Shakespeare Library. N.p., n.d. Web. 2014.
http://www.folger.edu/Content/Discover-Shakespeare/Shakespeares-Life/

Shakespeare's Globe. The Shakespeare Globe Trust, n.d. Web. 2014.
http://www.shakespearesglobe.com/education/discovery-space/fact-sheets

Shakespeare's Sonnets. Oxquarry Books Ltd, 2011. Web.
http://www.shakespeares-sonnets.com/

Encyclopedia Britannica's Guide to Shakespeare. Encyclopedia Britannica,
n.d. Web. 2014.
http://www.britannica.com/shakespeare/

No Fear Shakespeare. SparkNotes, 2014. Web.
http://nfs.sparknotes.com/

Green, Treye. "Shakespeare's 450th Birthday: 20 Facts About William
Shakespeare." International Business Times. N.p., n.d. Web. 22 Apr. 2014.
http://www.ibtimes.com/shakespeares-450th-birthday-20-facts-about-william-
shakespeare-1575062

"51 Random Facts About William Shakespeare." Random History. N.p.,
n.d. Web. 2009.
http://facts.randomhistory.com/2009/01/11_shakespeare.html

Hodin, Rachel. "12 Little-Known Facts About Shakespeare." Thought
Catalog. N.p., n.d. Web. 28 Aug. 2013.
http://thoughtcatalog.com/rachel-hodin/2013/08/12-little-known-facts-about-
shakespeare/

"William Shakespeare." Primary History. BBC News, n.d. Web. 2014.
http://www.bbc.co.uk/schools/primaryhistory/famouspeople/william_shake-
speare/

"Shakespeare FAQs." Shakespeare Birthplace Trust. N.p., n.d. Web. 2014.
http://www.shakespeare.org.uk/explore-shakespeare/faqs.html

Brown, Jessie. "10 Strange Facts about Shakespeare." Great British Mag.
N.p., n.d. Web. Apr. 2013.
http://greatbritishmag.co.uk/lifestyle/10-strange-facts-about-shakespeare

"10 Things You Didn't Know About William Shakespeare." History.com.
A&E Television, 16 July 2013. Web.
http://www.history.com/news/history-lists/10-things-you-didnt-know-about-
william-shakespeare

Wood, Michael. "The Shakespeare Paper Trail." BBC News. N.p., 17 Feb. 2011. Web.
http://www.bbc.co.uk/history/british/tudors/shakespeare_later_01.shtml

Spatola, Jamie. "The Quick 10: 10 Ways Shakespeare Changed Everything." Mental Floss. N.p., 2011. Web.
http://mentalfloss.com/article/29400/quick-10-10-ways-shakespeare-changed-everything

"Holy Trinity Church (Shakespeare's Tomb)." Frommer's. N.p., 2014. Web.
http://www.frommers.com/destinations/stratford-upon-avon/attractions/209563#sthash.VN7vSvF8.dpbs

"Did You Know....? William Shakespeare Edition." Art Works Blog. National Endowment for the Arts, 12 Apr. 2013. Web.
http://arts.gov/art-works/2013/did-you-know-happy-birthday-william-shakespeare-edition

Doran, Gregory. "Shakespeare: 10 Things You Didn't Know." The Telegraph. Telegraph Media Group, 22 Apr. 2014. Web.
http://www.telegraph.co.uk/culture/theatre/william-shakespeare/10755197/Shakespeare-10-things-you-didnt-know.html

Credits